gentleman?' Sabrina mocked unsteadily.

Sebastian's eyes had adjusted to the light but her face was a pale blur, her body less distinct. The compulsion to reach for her in the darkness was so strong the effort of fighting it made him quiver like someone with a fever. 'I deserved that—but you deserved a better proposal.'

'Not everyone has your way with words. I suspect the only proposals you have any working knowledge of are of the indecent variety.'

'I may not know much about duty, but you have now agreed to marry my brother and you are totally out of bounds. So you can stop looking at me like that.'

'You don't know how I'm looking at you.'

'I know those big hungry eyes. Just go inside while you still can.'

She shivered, a thrill of excitement shimmering through her body at the message in his dark voice. 'W... inside?'

Kim Lawrence lives on a farm in Anglesey with her university lecturer husband, assorted pets who arrived as strays and never left, and sometimes one or both of her boomerang sons. When she's not writing she loves to be outdoors gardening, or walking on one of the beaches for which the island is famous—along with being the place where Prince William and Catherine made their first home!

Visit the Author Profile page at millsandboon.co.uk for more titles.

A RING TO
SECURE HIS CROWN

BY
KIM LAWRENCE

First Published in Great Britain 2017
By Mills & Boon, an imprint of HarperCollins*Publishers*
1 London Bridge Street, London, SE1 9GF

© 2017 Kim Lawrence

ISBN: 978-0-263-92447-3

Our policy is to use papers that are natural, renewable and recyclable
products and made from wood grown in sustainable forests. The logging
and manufacturing processes conform to the legal environmental
regulations of the country of origin.

Printed and bound in Spain
by CPI, Barcelona

A RING TO
SECURE HIS CROWN

CHAPTER ONE

SABRINA CLOSED HER bedroom door with care, conscious of her two flatmates who were both doing a night rotation in Casualty. She had reached the front door, a piece of toast in one hand, her oversized bag in the other, when her phone rang.

She swore softly, and then again as her efforts at juggling caused her toast to land butter-side down on the carpet. Why did it *always* do that?

She dumped her bag, picked up the toast with a grimace and glanced at the caller ID before lifting the phone to her ear. The low-voiced conversation lasted a few moments as the junior lab assistant gave her the results she and the entire research team had been waiting for.

Consigning the toast to the waste-bin, Sabrina was smiling when she opened the door; the results were not what they had expected, they were better! Embracing the buzz of excitement, she hitched her bag over her shoulder, grabbed an apple from the fruit bowl to soothe her rumbling stomach and released the loose, heavy honey strands of hair that had got stuck down the collar of her jacket before backing out of the front door.

It was the noise that hit her first, like a solid wall

of sound; the voices calling her name seemed to come from everywhere.

Dropping the apple, she turned and was immediately blinded by flashing lights. She lifted a hand to shade her eyes and turned her head to avoid the microphones being thrust in her face.

Heart thudding like a piston, she tried to turn back but it was already too late. In seconds the weight of bodies pushing against her had already carried her several feet away and into the street and now she was surrounded.

'Lady Sabrina... Lady Sabrina... Lady Sabrina...! When is the wedding?'

'Will it happen before or after the island is reunified?'

'When did Prince Luis propose?'

'Is this a marriage of convenience?'

'What sort of message do you think you are sending to young women, Dr Summerville?'

The sound of her own name and the stream of questions coming from all directions felt like a physical assault. The conviction she had just walked into her own personal nightmare, the sense of galloping claustrophobia intensified along with the gut-freezing horror that literally paralyzed Sabrina. She couldn't breathe, she couldn't even think past the static buzz of panic in her head. She just closed her eyes, put her head down and waited for the ground to open up.

It didn't.

And then something did, though in amidst the confusion she didn't immediately register anything about what was happening until the grip on her wrist tightened and another hand slid around her waist. She was no longer being carried along by the media crush, she was being pulled in the opposite direction by someone who was strong enough to make it seem easy and to make her wild attempt to hit out at her abductor a joke.

It happened in a blur, one minute she was in the street trying to fight for her freedom and the next she was being unceremoniously dumped like a sack of potatoes into the back seat of a big sleek car that had been hidden from her view by the mass of bodies.

People didn't get kidnapped in front of the press and hundreds of cameras, she told herself while struggling to sit up. She managed it in time to see a camera being thrown at the crowd before the man who had climbed in beside her slammed the door on the noise outside. The mob were now pretty much hysterical.

'Drive, Charlie, if you would!' he drawled in an almost bored tone of voice.

The man in the driving seat reacted by doing just that. He pulled away from the kerb with a squeal of brakes and with scant regard for the lives of the bodies blocking their way.

Sabrina found her eyes connecting with the small, mean-looking eyes of the man in charge of the getaway in the rear-view mirror before she looked away. The tattoo in the shape of a dragon on the back of his thick neck was even less comforting.

Although she knew all about the physical and chemical processes that led the body to over-produce adrenaline, could answer, and actually *had* answered, an exam question on them, she had never, up to that point, personally experienced how compelling the flight-or-fight reflex was.

As the primitive survival response kicked in she literally threw herself at the door, pressing every button in a frantic effort to open it and sobbing with frustration when it didn't budge. She began to batter on the window, more in desperation than with any real hope of attracting attention—they were travelling at speed and the windows were blacked out.

'If you're trying to break it I should tell you that it's bulletproof, though that is quite a right hook you have, *cara*, and I consider myself lucky that you are not wearing heels.'

Her clenched fists slid down the glass and for a moment she rested her forehead against the coolness of the glass before she took a deep breath and turned to face her captor. She might have lost the fight to open the door but she'd won the fight to hide her fear behind a mask of cool disdain—well, as disdainful as you could look when your face was wet with tears and your mascara had most likely run.

'I am not your *cara*, I am not your anything, but if you don't let me go I will be your worst nightmare,' she promised. 'You will stop this car and let me out this instant or I will…' Her voice dried and her jaw hit her chest as she identified the man who was sitting in the corner, one arm resting along the padded backrest, the other holding a phone.

He smiled, looking like a fallen angel on performance-enhancing drugs. It had always made total sense to her that the devil would be good-looking or else where was the temptation?

Not that she was tempted in any way!

His electric-blue eyes glittering with amusement, Prince Sebastian Zorzi tipped his head and touched a gentle finger to her chin.

Shock zigzagged along her nerve endings as Sabrina pulled her head away breathing hard. The initial relief she'd felt upon realising she was not actually being abducted, but in fact rescued, was swallowed up by a wave of antipathy as she met the mockery in the eyes of her future brother-in-law. His suit was beautifully cut and a dark charcoal, the jacket stretched across broad shoulders, unbuttoned to reveal the white T-shirt he wore instead of a shirt and tie. The T-shirt clung just enough to suggest the strong, well-developed contours of his broad chest. It wasn't his tailoring that made her scalp tingle though—under the laconic surface there was an explosive quality about him. In the toughness stakes Sebastian Zorzi could have given the bulletproof glass a run for its money.

Obviously she had been aware that the brothers were physically dissimilar. Nothing surprising about that; siblings often were. She and Chloe looked nothing alike, after all.

But the Zorzi Princes were not just different, they were total opposites in everything. It went beyond their colouring or build, or even their smiles, actually *especially* their smiles! One's made you feel safe, the other? She gave a little shudder. *Safe* was not a word she could imagine many people using when it came to Sebastian Zorzi!

'That's right, Lady Sabrina, I'm the rescue party.' He lifted his hand and spoke into the phone cradled in his palm. Sabrina noticed his fingers were very long, the ends square-tipped and capable. They were definitely strong hands.

'Yes, I've got her. She's…' The dark lashes lifted from the angular jut of his high carved cheekbones, his blue eyes seemed to consider her for a moment—the bone-stripping intensity making her shift in her seat before he responded to the question she couldn't hear. 'In one piece, just about. She looks like she's been dragged through a hedge backwards, but she retains the ability to look down her well-bred little nose… So, yes, all right—if you like that sort of thing.'

His tone suggested that personally *he didn't like*, but then, having seen the sort of women Sebastian thought of as fine, Sabrina was actually quite glad.

He had a type.

And it had nothing to do with IQ points.

Hard to imagine that the endless succession of tall, leggy blondes whose names had been linked with his were universally dumb, but Sabrina had always imagined, with an uncharacteristic lack of charity, that they probably pretended to be dim! There was a type of man who just couldn't cope with a woman who could challenge them intellectually, and in her opinion the black sheep of the Zorzi family ticked all the boxes for that type!

He was the sort of royal prince who made republicans say smugly, *I told you so*…or they should do, she reflected grimly. It was just that somehow Sebastian made the unacceptable seem charming and no matter what his indiscretions everyone seemed to forgive him; and not only that, they *liked* him despite the fact he'd been sticking a finger up to authority all of his adult life.

It had always mystified Sabrina. Yet sitting a few feet away from him in an enclosed space, she began to understand it better. He didn't have to deliver a charm offensive, he just had to breathe!

The sensual shock wave of his presence had to be experienced to be believed! She had, and Sabrina no longer believed that any of the stories that circulated about him were exaggerated.

In the past it would not have been strange that they had never met. For many years relations between the two Velatian royal families had been, if not frigid, definitely cool.

Times had changed. No longer enemies, the two royal families had become the best of friends and co-conspirators, united in a common cause.

But at every social occasion where both families had been present, somehow Sebastian had always been absent. In fact, it wouldn't surprise her if Sebastian had been banned from such occasions. The only time Sabrina had even been in the same room as Sebastian Zorzi previously, it had been a very large room and he had vanished very early in the evening through a back exit, along with the much younger wife of an elderly diplomat, before they'd had the chance to be formally introduced.

Later that same evening she remembered the awe-inspiring and rather cold, or so it had always seemed to her, King Ricard coming to find his younger son. Luis, she recalled, had covered for his brother. It seemed to be the pattern of the siblings' relationship, his brother breaking the rules and Luis covering up for him.

If that meeting had ever happened she might have been prepared for the aura of raw masculinity Sebastian projected like a force field. It was primitive, raw sex appeal in its most concentrated form.

It made her skin prickle, her heart race and her limbs grow heavy and shakily weak. She didn't like it, but she accepted that she might well be in the minority there. A lot, if not most, might not exactly disapprove of the blatant sexuality of his wide, mobile mouth and the hard sculpted lines of his face. She took comfort in the knowledge that any second-year medical student, or, for that matter, sensible person, would have known her symptoms were caused by the after-effects of shock.

'Did anyone see us leave…?' He repeated the mystery caller's question. 'A few, I'd say.' His eyes, glittering with malicious amusement, found her own and she stopped the frenzied smoothing of her hair while he responded to the person on the other end of the line. 'I wasn't actually counting, but, no, she didn't give them any quotes, barring the curses. I learnt a few new ones!' He winced and lifted the phone away from his ear, waiting a moment, a smile playing across his lips until eventually he pressed it back into the angle of his jaw. 'Of course I'm not being serious. She was the epitome of inbred princess cool,' he soothed, before sliding the phone back into the breast pocket of his jacket.

Sabrina still didn't really know what was happening, but in that moment her desire to find out came second to her desire to react to his comments. 'The next time you accuse someone of being *inbred* I think maybe you should consult your own family tree.'

He gave a low throaty chuckle that alarmingly raised goosebumps over the surface of her skin. 'Point taken, though, as I'm sure you are aware, there was for some time a question mark over my genetic inheritance.'

Her eyes fell even though he displayed none of the awkwardness she immediately felt. Of course she knew. News of the late Queen's affair had found its way onto every front page after the love letters she had written to her lover had found their way into the public domain after the man's death.

Then soon after, in case anyone had missed the lurid headlines, there was the book written by the man's ex-wife and the nanny, who had been the first to connect the dates with the birth of the Queen's second son and shared her suspicions with a tabloid.

There had been a show of solidarity by the Zorzi royal family at the time too. The Queen had appeared looking beautiful and frail at the side of her husband, the two Princes with their hair slicked back and faces shiny.

'But nobody believes that now,' Sabrina said uncomfortably.

He threw her a sardonic look. 'Oh, plenty believe it, *cara*, and a lot more wish it was true…' One slanted brow arched as he shrugged his shoulders. 'Myself included.'

Distracted from her own situation by this statement, she could not hide her astonishment. 'You *wish* you were a bastard? I'm sorry, I…' She broke off, blushing furiously, but Sebastian Zorzi did not appear even slightly put out by being referred to as a bastard.

'Let's just say I don't wake up feeling lucky that Zorzi blood is running through my veins.'

'Well, Luis is proud of his heritage,' she countered defensively.

'My brother is more forgiving than I am.'

'Forgiving of who?'

The mockery left his eyes as he stared at her for a long moment. The expression on his face was hard to read. 'While I'm enjoying this deep and meaningful discussion, aren't there other questions you should be asking at this moment?'

She shook her head in confusion.

'Like, what just happened?'

She immediately felt stupid. 'So what did just happen?'

He gave a throaty chuckle that sounded cruel to Sabrina. 'Welcome to the rest of your life, *cara*.'

'I'm not spending the rest of my life with you.' Or even another second, if she had her way.

'My loss, I'm sure,' he drawled sarcastically.

She clenched her teeth. 'But *why* the cameras? The journalists? I don't understand.'

His dark brows lifted. 'Really? I'd heard you were bright. Ah, well, bright doesn't always equate with quick on the uptake, I suppose,' he conceded as she flushed angrily. 'There has been a leak.'

Crazily, all she could think about with those blue eyes mocking her was the leak in her bathroom that had occurred last winter, the one that had taken the landlord a month to fix.

He sighed, the sound the auditory equivalent of an eye roll. It was the last straw for Sabrina.

'Look, I'm sure having cameras and microphones thrust in your face is all part of a normal day in your life but it's not in mine, so shall we *pretend* just for a moment that you have an ounce of sensitivity? I'm badly traumatised and, like you said, not so quick on the uptake!'

A tense silence followed her outburst. *She never yelled!*

'Ever heard of volume control?'

She said nothing, afraid if she opened her mouth again she'd do something even more embarrassing like cry.

As he stared at her the humorous glint in his eyes completely faded, though there was certainly no softening in his blunt delivery as he spelt out the situation. 'Someone in the inner circle sold the story: wedding, reunification, the whole master plan.'

She shook her head and swallowed past the lump the size of a tennis ball that was lodged in her throat 'Why would anyone do that?'

'Oh, I don't know, maybe for *money*?'

She gnawed on her full lower lip, resenting the ease with which he made her feel gauche and naive.

'But don't worry, we know it wasn't you.'

Her eyes flew wide, the pallor that emphasised the sprinkling of freckles across the bridge of her small straight nose deepening. *'What?'*

'Well, first thought was that you might have got tired of waiting for Luis to pop the question and decided to nudge things along.'

'Why the hell would I want to do that?' In the hot-house emotional atmosphere her knee-jerk reaction emerged uncensored. 'I mean...' Her eyes fell from his searing stare. No, he couldn't see what was in her head; how the hell could he? At that moment *she* didn't even know what was in her head.

'I touched a nerve...interesting.'

'I am not a science experiment!'

One side of his mouth lifted in an incredibly attractive half-smile that made her fight to catch her breath while her skin prickled with antagonism.

'I am sensing that this is bad timing?'

'I don't know what you're talking about.' The bad timing was the twisting sensation in her stomach.

'No need to be coy. I'm assuming that there is a boyfriend in the wings you want to break the news to? Does this guy know that you've been tagged as a sacrifice to the great cause of reunification for years?'

'I am not a sacrifice!'

'Sorry, a willing victim, then. How many barrels of oil do you reckon marrying my brother is worth, just an estimate?'

She clenched her teeth. 'I am *not* a victim—'

'And the oil deposits in your rocky little kingdom

have nothing whatsoever to do with the sudden enthusiasm to reunify our lovely island state? Sorry, not actually *sudden*. How old were you when they told you the plan? That the feel-good factor of a royal wedding would silence the traditionalists on both sides of the border who cling to the good old days when we hated each other's guts.' He pushed his broad, muscular shoulders a little deeper into the leather backrest and let his head fall back. 'It must make you feel very special to know that you make up an entire chapter in a legal document that took two countries ten years to agree on.'

'You forgot one important factor...my family ran out of male heirs and, for the record, *some* guts,' she told him with grim sincerity, 'are easier to hate than others.'

His head lifted; he was grinning his insanely attractive smile. 'Go ahead,' he invited, tossing her his phone, which she caught on instinct. 'I'll pretend to be deaf.'

Lips clamped tight, she tossed it back. 'Thanks but I have my own phone and I don't have a boyfriend.' At university she'd dated a bit, but nothing serious, and then her best friend had met, fallen for and got engaged to a fellow student all in the space of a month. And though Sabrina could not imagine finding herself similarly smitten she had asked herself, *what if*?

Did she really want to find her soul mate only to be forced to walk away from him? The anger she hadn't even acknowledged to herself at the time suddenly found its voice—its *loud* voice.

'I don't date. You go on dates to hopefully get butterflies wondering if he is *the one*, right? So what would be the point?' She stopped, bringing her lashes down in a concealing curtain across her eyes, appalled as much by the bitter outburst as the person she had chosen to open up to. 'Besides, I've been far too busy with work for much else.'

'And now you're going to give that up too like a good little girl, anxious to please. I can see now why it never actually crossed anyone's mind that you were the leak. The general consensus being that you have never broken a rule in your life.'

His scorn stung, even if what he claimed was depressingly true. She had always been the good girl; she was not about to apologise for it. 'You make that sound like a vice.'

'As opposed to what…a *virtue*?' On the point of answering his own blighting question, he seemed to change his mind when after a short static pause he added, in an oddly flat voice, 'The culprit—and, *mea culpa*, he is one of ours—has been found, and he is, as we speak, being dealt with severely.'

'Dealt with?' It sounded sinister, especially when Sebastian said it.

His grin reappeared but it didn't reach his blue eyes. 'Don't worry, despite the bad press we get we haven't actually executed anyone for a century or so, as for thumbscrews we have found them not really that effective, so we just sacked him.'

'He lost his job?'

The air escaped through his clenched teeth in an irritated hiss. 'You're worried about the fate of a man who was responsible for throwing you to the wolves back there? Wow, you really are going to have to toughen up if you're joining our family, sweetheart!' he ground out. 'But if it makes you feel better the guy won't be penniless. His insider story of what goes on behind closed doors is pretty much guaranteed to make the bestseller list after it has been serialised in the Sunday papers.'

The colour that had been seeping back into her face retreated. 'That's terrible!'

'But hardly news,' he responded, sounding very relaxed about the situation. 'The fact my stepmother has a plastic surgeon on speed dial is not exactly the best-kept secret, neither is my father's tendency to throw the first thing that comes to hand when thwarted.'

It crossed Sabrina's mind that an outsider's view of the place could not be any more jaundiced than this cynical insider's.

'So what actually happens now?'

'Now you go get measured for your wedding dress.' His gaze slid down her body.

Smiling through clenched teeth, Sabrina struggled not to react to the calculated insolence in his scrutiny, sweat breaking out across her upper lip as she fought the impulse to lift a hand to shield her shamefully hardened nipples.

'Size eight, am I right? Or maybe a ten up top and an eight in the hips?' His eyes dropped to her legs where her ankles were neatly crossed one over the other, making her aware that she was rhythmically rubbing one calf against the other.

The abrupt cessation of movement brought his heavy-lidded gaze back to her face. 'I'm curious—did it ever occur to you to say no?'

'*No?*' she echoed, wondering if any woman ever had to say no to him. It seemed very unlikely.

Her sense of disorientation increased as his eyes narrowed on her face. 'Or are you actually content to be a pawn?'

'I don't know what you're talking about.'

'Really? Next you'll be telling me that you love Luis, that he is *the one*.'

Her full lips thinned as she framed a carefully expressionless response to his contemptuous question. 'I'm not going to tell *you* anything…' Then spoilt the effect by instantly exploding resentfully, 'I wouldn't expect someone like *you* to understand.'

Sebastian levered his shoulders from the leather padded backrest and seat as he leaned forward, angling his body towards her. 'And what exactly wouldn't someone *like me* understand?'

She clamped her lips and shook her head, not that the action lessened the feeling of being cornered or the nerve-rattling impact of the aura of testosterone he exuded. If the option to crawl out of her skin had been offered at that moment she would have taken it.

'Duty,' she choked through clenched teeth.

His throaty laugh was mockingly ironic. 'Of course, *duty*.' His slow hand clap raised the levels of her animosity.

'What is funny about that?'

He widened his eyes. 'Sorry,' he said, sounding anything but. 'Was I meant to look impressed by your sacrifice? Oh, I don't think it's funny, *cara*, I think it's *tragic* that you are embracing martyrdom so enthusiastically. I'd blame the brainwashing but I think perhaps you were always the *good* little girl.'

The air left her lungs in a wrathful hiss. 'I have grown up, unlike *some* people, and I do not consider myself a martyr!' Her voice wavered; she was trembling inside and out with the violent rush of emotions his words had shaken loose.

It was a fact of life—or at least *her* life—that she had little control over a lot of things, but this was one occasion when she didn't have to take it—*or* him!

'You can mock the concept of duty and service, but

I'd prefer to be a good girl, as you put it, than a selfish, thrill-seeking, hedonistic waste of space. Has there ever been a moment in your life when you haven't put yourself and your pleasure above anything else?'

She probably imagined the flash of something that had looked like admiration before his head tilted to one side as he gave the appearance of considering her question. 'Probably not,' he conceded.

'Well, being a selfish waster is not a luxury we can all have even if we wanted it.'

'You enjoy your occupation of the moral high ground and in a few years' time, when you are wearing the crown, I just hope you will still think it was worth the things you gave up.'

'I haven't given anything up.'

'How about your work? Why did you waste time, effort and money to qualify as a doctor when you had no intention of ever using that skill?'

Her eyes fell. 'Research is important.'

'Granted, but it will have to survive without you, because my instructions are to deliver you to the embassy. Ours.'

'I'm not a parcel, I'm a person!'

'With feelings, of course—where are my manners? The shoulder to cry on…' He leaned towards her and her nostrils flared as the male, warm scent of his body, mingled with a faint fragrance, filled them. 'Feel free.'

'I do not require a shoulder and if I did—'

'I'm only the spare,' he cut in with an exaggerated sigh as she leaned heavily back. 'I get that totally. You're saving yourself for the man with the crown.'

Her hands clenched into fists as she looked at him with burning eyes. 'You are a really horrible man, you know that?'

'And you are a very beautiful woman.' A look of incredulity flickered across his face. 'Wait, are you…?' He put a finger to her chin and lifted her face towards him. 'Yes, you're blushing!'

'I am *not* blushing.' A sudden possibility had occurred to her, one that would explain his outrageous attitude and the reckless gleam in his eyes. 'Have you been drinking?'

'Not for at least two hours.' He raised his voice to reach the man in the driver's seat. 'Charlie, what time did we leave?'

'I believe it was four a.m., sir,' the man with the tattoo responded in a cultured voice.

'Really? Oh, well, I'm totally sober…well, maybe not totally,' he conceded. 'Oh, here we are.' The car drew up outside the embassy. 'Oh, and I almost forgot, Luis sent his love, and this.'

He leaned across and the sudden shock that had held her immobile as his lips covered hers faded into something else as the slow, sensuous exploration deepened. Sabrina was not sure how her arms came to be around Sebastian's neck but they were, and she was kissing him back as if he were water and she'd spent the last week in the desert. She had never before felt, never imagined anything like the sudden explosion of hot need inside her.

A need that intensified as she felt a shudder move through his lean body and felt the touch of his tongue between her parted lips. She moaned into his mouth and pushed her body into his as he kneaded his fingers into her hair. She felt on fire, filled with an aching need to…*what*?

Luckily, before she found the answer, as suddenly as it had started the kiss stopped.

She sat there, shivering, eyes wide, sucking in air in tiny laboured gasps as he leaned back in the seat staring at her, his hypnotic blue stare searing. Hot, dark streaks of colour emphasising the contours of his sharp cheekbones.

'How dare you?' The sound of her open palm making contact with his cheek was shocking.

He lifted a hand to his cheek and drawled, 'Don't slap the messenger, *cara*.'

'You are vile!' She choked, almost falling out of the car when the door was opened by someone wearing a military uniform.

She could hear his laughter as she walked stiffly up the shallow flight of embassy steps.

CHAPTER TWO

SEBASTIAN SET HIS shoulder to the stiff door that opened out onto a small Juliet balcony. It gave suddenly, filling the warm room with a welcome breeze. The view was as dramatic as the plumbing was idiosyncratic. His shower had run cold and then it had almost scalded him. Oh, well, maybe it was time he learnt how the other half lived, even if that half could claim a heritage as illustrious as his own, such as it was.

For a moment his lip curled into a cynical smile. For reasons obvious when you considered his nickname at school had been *the royal bastard*, Sebastian had never been able to take the whole heritage thing seriously.

A tap on the door made him turn, but before he could respond Luis walked into the room, his normal smile absent.

'Reading your body language I'd guess you were just told you've got weeks to live, or you've just had a heart to heart with our father. How is His Royal Highness?'

Luis's heavy sigh and despondent attitude would normally have evoked a sympathetic reaction from Sebastian, but today the only thing he felt was a surge of irritation. Didn't Luis realise that until he showed a bit of backbone the King was never going to stop trying to micromanage his life? Maybe not even then, Sebastian, a realist, conceded. If he were in his brother's shoes…

But you're not, are you, Seb?

Luis gets the crown and the girl.

'I didn't think you'd come, neither did…anyone.'

'You asked.'

Actually his father had ordered, which under normal circumstances would have guaranteed Sebastian's non-appearance, and yet he was here. *So why?* He rubbed the towel across his dripping hair and veered away from the question in his head before it formed.

'I asked the last three times I came to visit the Summervilles.'

'You know I have an allergy to duty.'

'So you keep telling everyone. Seriously—'

'It is a very serious allergy.'

'I wanted you to get to know Sabrina.'

'It's you she's marrying.' *And me she's kissing,* he thought, the sharp twinge of guilt he felt drowned out by the stronger slug of lusty heat that accompanied the memory of those soft, sweet-tasting lips. If Luis had kissed her more often maybe she wouldn't have melted in his arms.

That's right, Seb, because it's never your fault, is it?

He waited for the familiar hit of mingled frustration, sympathy and affection as he watched Luis walk, shoulders hunched in defeat, across the room. Instead, Sebastian found himself feeling anger and something that, had the circumstances been different, he would have called envy.

But of course it wasn't.

Envy would mean that his brother had something that he wanted, and Luis didn't.

Luis was welcome to the crown.

There *had* been a time when they were growing up that being pushed into the background and being referred to as the *spare* had got to Sebastian, but that had been before he had recognised that it was a lot worse for Luis, carrying the expectations of a country on his young shoulders. Luis had no choices—even his wife was picked out for him.

Luis was welcome to his bride; Sebastian had his freedom. His father had told both of his sons that privilege came with a price; well, so far he'd been proving his father wrong. Sebastian enjoyed the privileges that came with his title without any of the responsibilities.

And Sebastian didn't want to marry Sabrina—he didn't want to marry anyone—he just wanted to take her to bed. Even thinking about her now, and that miracle of a mouth of hers, made smoky desire slither hotly through him.

He ignored it. He'd kissed Sabrina and he wasn't going to do it again, even if the primal attraction that drew him to this woman was stronger than anything he could ever remember feeling. He knew himself well enough to know that it would pass—it always did.

And in the meantime there were plenty of women to kiss who were not about to marry his brother, who were not about to throw away their lives. *Her* business, he reminded himself, *her* choice.

Luckily he had recognised, before the entire kiss incident in the car had got out of perspective, the real danger of building it up into something it was not. She had an incredible mouth, beautiful lips and they made him hungry. The need to taste had swept away every other consideration in his head, but it had been what it was: a 'perfect storm' moment. Or maybe a perfect moment of madness, fuelled by the alcohol he'd imbibed much earlier in the morning at the nightclub, where he had been even more bored than usual.

The chances were, seeing Sabrina here, in her natural environment, as a woman who represented everything he had been rebelling against and rejecting all his life, that he would regain his normal objectivity.

'I didn't expect you to come, but I'm glad you did. I do appreciate the support.'

'Support?' Sebastian queried with a frown.

'I can't say I'm exactly looking forward to tonight.'

'Performance anxiety or…don't tell me you're having second thoughts?'

Luis turned away but not quickly enough to hide his flush of annoyance at the joke that presumably offended his highly developed sense of duty. If it *was* annoyance?

Guilt? Could he have hit a nerve? Was his brother having second thoughts? Sebastian dismissed the possibility almost straight away, no matter what his personal feelings. For Luis, duty, no matter what form it took, came first.

'So how is the blushing bride?'

'Fine… I guess.'

'You guess? You mean you didn't spend the night saying hello?' Sebastian said, immediately imagining himself saying a very long hello.

'I only just arrived and she…we… She doesn't blush.'

Sebastian's brows lifted. 'Oh?' he said, remembering the delicious rosy tinge that had washed over Sabrina's pale skin.

'Not that that is a *bad* thing.'

Sebastian's eyes narrowed in his brother's face. 'Which means that *you* think it is.'

Luis looked guilty. 'She just isn't always what you'd call very spontaneous.'

Sebastian cloaked his expression as he heard the echo of that soft little mewling cry as she'd opened her mouth to him. His body hardened helplessly at the memory of her soft breasts pushing into his ribcage.

The effort of fighting his way free of those intrusive memories delayed his response. 'Spontaneity can be overrated.' It could also be great...*she* would be great in bed.

Never going to find out, Seb.

He was a bastard but not *that* much of a bastard.

'Exactly, especially when your every move is being scrutinised. She has all the qualities to make the perfect Queen.'

The speculative furrow between Sebastian's dark brows deepened as he listened to his brother, sounding very much like a man who was trying desperately to convince himself that he believed in what he was saying.

'I'm sold,' he murmured drily. 'How about you?'

Luis dodged the soft question and his brother's speculative stare. 'Marriage is all about teamwork.'

'So I hear.' He had never given marriage much thought aside from concluding fairly early on that it was not for him, about the same time that he had nearly made a fatal error. 'I nearly proposed once,' he remembered, a rueful smile tugging the corners of his mouth upwards as he tried and failed to visualise the face of the woman who he had decided, at nineteen, was the love of his life.

'*You!*' His brother's jaw hit his chest before he recovered. '*You've* been in love?' Luis shook his head. 'Who? When? What happened?'

'What always happens—the glitter rubs off. I found out she snored and her laugh grated, but for a while I believed that she was perfect. Actually, I've believed quite a few were perfect since, the difference being I no longer expect it to last.'

In Sebastian's opinion, if you were looking for a formula for unhappiness it would be hard to come up with a more sure-fire method than tying yourself to one person for life based on a short-lived chemical high.

'Perfect? Like you, you mean?'

Sebastian winced and grinned, watching as Luis, his expression growing distracted, moved to one of the two chairs arranged at the foot of the bed. Sebastian held up a warning hand.

'I wouldn't do that. I made the same mistake. The leg dropped off. I've propped it.'

Luis made a detour to the other chair.

Sebastian's gaze moved around the room of faded grandeur. 'It's not what I was expecting. They really are strapped for cash. No wonder,' he observed cynically, 'they are so willing to sell their daughter off to the highest bidder.'

'They're not selling her!' Luis protested. 'Sabrina understands. She respects—'

'Our mother understood,' Sebastian interrupted, wondering if the anger he felt would ever go away. Anger at the system that had trapped his mother in a marriage that had, in the end, destroyed her. 'And that didn't turn out so well.'

'It's not the same!' his brother protested, flushing as he surged to his feet.

Sebastian arched a brow. 'From where I'm standing it looks like a classic case of history repeating itself.'

Luis's horrified rebuttal was immediate. 'I'm not like…him.'

Then break the blasted cycle!

Sebastian didn't voice his thought. What would be the point? He knew his brother would never challenge their father, and, if the positions were reversed, was he so damned sure that he would? Easy to criticise from where he stood.

'I wonder, Seb. What do you think he'd do if he knew...?'

Sebastian's irritation slipped away as he walked across to where his brother stood and laid a hand on Luis's shoulder. 'He won't,' he said firmly. 'We burnt the letters. No one knows they ever existed.'

The young brothers had not known at the time they discovered the love letters hidden under a floorboard that despite breaking off the affair after she discovered she was carrying her lover's child she had continued to see him after the child she had conceived with him had been born.

The irony was that they were right, there was a royal bastard, only it wasn't the son that the scandal-mongers had identified.

'As far as the world is concerned, the affair only started the year I was born.' Sebastian could see no reason anyone should ever know. 'We are the only two people who know, unless you plan on telling him?'

Luis shuddered. 'I stood by and watched you being bullied at school and then at home when we both know that you should be King. I have no legitimate claim to the throne. I'm not even his son.'

Sebastian shook his head. 'Be glad of that every day. Be glad of it, Luis!' he said, his voice gruff with ferocious sincerity. 'You've escaped the taint that I carry. *I'm* the son the bastard deserves. You will make a better King than I ever could be. You're the one who has made all the sacrifices...and you are still making them.' Sebastian straightened up, relaxing the grip on his brother's shoulders. 'You don't *have* to marry her, you know. You could say no.'

Luis shook his head and dodged his brother's gaze. 'Easy for you to say. I'm not—'

'Selfish as hell?' Sebastian thought of where being unselfish had got his mother. He'd choose selfish every time.

Luis's gaze lifted, just as his brother vanished into the bathroom. 'I'm not a rebel like you. I need to... I *care* about what people think about me.'

Sebastian re-emerged with a fresh towel, which he rubbed vigorously over his damp hair.

'And this marriage isn't about me, it's about bigger things. I'm realistic about it.'

'So how does *she* feel about it?'

Luis gave an uncomprehending shrug. 'How do you mean?'

'I mean what does *Sabrina* expect from this marriage? Is she realistic too?' He gave a sudden shrug, annoyed with himself for wasting time on a subject that was none of his business. 'Is the warm glow of doing the right thing enough for her too?' He began to vigorously rub his already towel-dried hair, asking himself where this swell of outrage was coming from. She'd made her bed and she seemed happy to lie in it...with his brother. 'Hell, Luis, do you two even talk?'

'We have a lifetime to talk,' Luis responded, not sounding as though the life he saw stretching ahead filled him with joy. 'But you mean sex, don't you? It's not like you to be so squeamish. Actually no, I haven't slept with her.'

'That's not what I meant, but as you've shared aren't

you taking this untouched virgin bride stuff a bit too far, Luis?'

Luis laughed. 'Even father doesn't expect that.'

'How incredibly liberal-minded of him.' Sebastian was still struggling with the implication of some of Sabrina's unguarded comments. Was it *really* possible that Sabrina had not had a lover, out of *fear* of falling in love?

'What if you're not compatible? Have you thought of that?'

Luis for once looked annoyed. 'For God's sake, Seb, this isn't about how good she is in bed!'

As the comment unlocked a stream of graphic images that flowed relentlessly through his head, Sebastian lowered his eyelids to half-mast. His jaw clenched as he struggled to stem the flow and pretended an amusement he was a long way from feeling. 'But it would help.'

It would help him even more, Sebastian mused darkly, if he could stop thinking of unfastening glossy honey hair and watching it fall over bare shoulders, pushing it back to reveal small firm breasts...

Oblivious to the tension underpinning his brother's taut delivery, Luis laughed. 'I really like her.'

'Like?'

Luis tipped his head in acknowledgment. 'She's sweet,' he began with the attitude of a man who was clutching at straws.

'And,' he ploughed on with determination, 'she has a lot of common sense.'

Were they even talking about the same woman? Sebastian wondered, thinking about the woman who had attempted to punch her way out of his locked car just to avoid being shut in there with him.

He recognised she'd been driven to this drastic move by desperation and fear and he had fully intended saying something to soothe her, but the expression on her face when she'd recognised him, the fact that she'd looked as though she had just discovered she had jumped into a car beside the Devil himself...he simply hadn't been able to resist playing up to her prejudices a little.

But then she had challenged his own firmly embedded prejudices. In the abstract he had been able to despise Sabrina Summerville, or at least the *idea* of her, a woman who, despite coming from a different generation, was just as willing as his own mother had been to be a compliant, political pawn.

The first surprise had been the desire that had twisted inside him when he'd found himself sitting just inches away from her, which shouldn't have happened. He had seen the photos. He already knew that she was good-looking, admittedly more classy than classically beautiful. But what those photos had not prepared him for was the crystal clarity of her skin, the sprinkling of freckles across the bridge of her small straight nose, the deep liquid darkness of her eyes that seemed to reflect her every mood like a mirror. And last, but definitely not least, the pink lushness of her amazing lips.

The blood-roaring primal intensity of his reaction had effectively blocked everything else from his mind for what might only have been seconds, but could have been an hour.

And the hits had just kept coming!

He'd expected a passive victim; he had got a feisty fighter, who clearly thought he was a total waste of space. What had got to him the most had been the conflict in her eyes, her vulnerability.

He'd just wanted to tell her not to do it. Not to marry

Luis. Instead he'd kissed her…a greedy response to a need that had been visceral in its intensity.

'I've never seen her lose her temper,' Luis said.

Sebastian could not control the bark of laughter that bubbled up from his chest as he lifted a hand to his cheek where the imprint of her fingers had lasted, but he didn't react to his brother's puzzled look.

'Perhaps you should try giving her cause and see what happens?'

'She's very pretty,' Luis added, his tone almost defensive as though he expected his brother to deny the fact.

Was Luis serious? The woman was beautiful. She wasn't his type, he had never leaned in the direction of cut-glass delicacy, but even *he* could recognise her natural beauty, the rare 'get out of bed with her hair mussed and still look knockout gorgeous' beauty, not that he would ever get the chance to prove his theory.

She was his brother's.

The reminder slowed the heat rising inside him but did not stop its slow, inexorable progress.

What are you, Seb? Fifteen? Get a grip, man!

'Are you asking me for an opinion?' Sebastian struggled hard to tap into the sympathy he normally felt for his brother, who was the one expected to make a marriage of convenience, the one looking ahead to a life of being the acceptable public face of the crown.

'No, yes? I suppose?' His brother produced one of his genuine smiles, seeming to suddenly shrug off his mood with an ease that Sebastian envied.

'Maybe you should go on a date.'

'With *Sabrina*?'

'Well, the dating ritual is kind of what people do before they get married, unless you have one of those "wake up in Vegas with a tattoo, a hangover and a wife" marriages. I can recommend the first two as a way of passing a weekend.'

Luis's eyes slid from his brother's as he sketched a smile. 'I haven't thanked you yet, for getting her out of that press scrum.'

'Glad to be of help,' Sebastian said, wondering about the change of subject and his brother's unusually evasive attitude. Luis, he decided as he studied his brother's face, looked positively shifty.

'I'm sure she took it all in her stride.'

Sebastian clamped his jaw as he fought a compulsion to defend Sabrina from the criticism he could hear behind this faint praise. 'You'd have preferred she'd have fallen apart?'

'Of course not.'

'Actually she was pretty shaken, but she came out fighting.' He saw no point adding that the fight had been mostly directed, quite deservedly, at him.

Luis got to his feet. 'She was lucky you were so close.'

'She might not agree… I'd been drinking.'

Luis looked amused. 'Fall asleep and snore, did you?'

Sebastian's eyes fell. 'Not exactly.'

Sabrina stubbornly refused to acknowledge the lump in her throat as she unpacked. The task didn't take long. There wasn't much, just a few pieces of clothing and personal items she had hastily crammed into a holdall.

They represented the majority of her things from the London flat she'd shared with a couple of girlfriends, or *had* up until two days ago.

The embassy staff hadn't wanted her to return at all that day, but in the end she'd been given the begrudging go-ahead for half an hour with what they'd termed a *discreet* security presence, which had turned out to consist of a team of four large dark-suited men.

Sabrina had retained enough of her natural sense of irony—*just*—to wonder what *non*-discreet looked like, as two of the silent, unsmiling figures had stared straight ahead as she'd packed and written a note for her flatmates, who had both been sleeping after a long night shift. The other two minders had been, as they'd put it, *securing the exits…* She really didn't want to know what that involved! Though the dawning realisation that soon this bizarre would be her normal had made her lose whatever humour she might have seen in the situation.

When it had come to making a goodbye visit to the research unit where she had worked for just over the last year she'd changed tack, not requesting permission, instead just announcing her intention the next morning. Wait, no, it had been *this* morning. Things were happening so fast it was a struggle to retain any sense of time in this speeded-up version of her own life. She had hidden her surprise when the tactic had worked. Perhaps in the future she should stop saying please and simply demand?

Being the future Queen had to have some benefits.

You're getting ahead of yourself, Brina. You're not even a princess yet.

Her ironic grin barely surfaced before it vanished, because *soon* she *would* be.

She supposed she didn't really have the right to feel so shocked, it was hardly news, but in the past it had been a distant thing. Now it was all *very* real and there was no more pretending that her life was normal.

An expression of impatience drifted across her heart-shaped face, firming the lines of her delicate jaw and soft full lips as she cut off the self-pitying direction of her thoughts.

It is what it is, Brina, so get over it, she told herself sternly as she shook out the silky blouse she was clutching and put it on a hanger.

Was it actually worth the effort of unpacking?

The rate at which things were moving now would mean this wouldn't be her home for much longer. They were talking June wedding. Weeks away, not months or years. Once more she stubbornly ignored the flurry in her belly, less butterflies and more a buzzard's wings flapping this time in the pit of her stomach.

Her determined composure wobbled, as did her lower lip, as she pulled out the last item. The outline of the white lab coat she held up blurred as her dark eyes filled with hot tears.

She dashed a hand impatiently across the dampness on her cheeks and blinked hard as her thoughts were inexorably dragged back to when the colleagues she had worked beside for the past year had given her an impromptu leaving party. Some party poppers left from New Year had been pulled from a drawer and dutifully popped, exciting a mild overreaction from the security men, one of whom had flung her to the floor.

Someone whose name she didn't even know was willing to put himself between her and a bullet. She could see the surreal realisation hit her friends almost as hard as it did her.

In the subsequent dampened party atmosphere someone had handed around sausage rolls hastily bought from the twenty-four-hour mini-mart on the corner, and then they had presented her with the lab coat, a crown emblem sewn onto the breast pocket.

She had struggled to smile at the joke while accepting the leaving present and hugs of colleagues, who'd all said how much they were going to miss her, while she had tried hard not to think about how much she would miss them. She'd miss, too, the challenge of her work—unlike the challenges that lay ahead, this one had been of her own choosing.

Despite the hugs she'd been able to see they were looking at her differently, *thinking* about her differently. The realisation had saddened but not surprised her. Experience had taught her to expect no less. It was why once she'd had a choice in such things she had never advertised her title or background. She'd wanted to be accepted for who she was with no preconceptions.

She would always treasure her time at university, both as a medical student and then staff member at the prestigious research unit. Dr Summerville was a title she had earned and was proud of. *Lady* Sabrina, daughter of the Duke and Duchess of East Vela, was simply an accident of birth, the same accident that would see her promotion to Princess and one day Queen of the soon-to-be-reunified island kingdom.

She had relished the opportunity to be judged for her ability and not who her parents were. She had liked that when people had asked her where she was from, *East Vela* had drawn a puzzled frown and an inevitable, *where is that?* Or, *don't you mean Vela Main?*

There were big advantages for someone who did not like attention of being a royal from somewhere so obscure, the main one being that a third-division royal did not rate heavy security—one of those things she was learning that you did not fully appreciate until it vanished.

For the last few years Velatian politics had seemed a long way away, and she had kept it there, enjoying her freedom, her taste of real life. Sure, she'd been able to hear the clock ticking down, and the knowledge of what lay ahead had never vanished, but she had always known that her parents would make sure she was eased gently into her future role.

But there had been no gentle easing, more like a total immersion. A sink-or-swim introduction of what it meant to be Queen-in-waiting.

One day she had gone to bed as Dr Summerville, an invisible white coat in a laboratory, and had walked out into the street the next morning to calls of, *'Lady Sabrina, when is the wedding?'*

Her eyes clouded with memories as she rubbed her arm where the imprint of his fingers was beginning to turn from black to a more mellow yellow. She squeezed her eyes shut but couldn't block out his face…or her guilt, or the feeling in the pit of her stomach when she remembered how his mouth had felt against hers, his taste, the raw sexual energy he exuded.

She lifted both hands to her head and yelled, 'Go away!'

'Why? What have I done?' Sabrina's eyes flew open as her sister walked into the room and flung herself face down on the bed.

'There's a wasp…do you mind?' Sabrina said, pretending a crossness she didn't feel because she was glad to see her sister. She eased a dress out from under Chloe's prone form. 'I am wearing this tonight.'

Chloe propped her chin on her steepled fingers and scanned the garment that Sabrina hung on a coat hanger and hooked over her wardrobe door.

Chloe gave her verdict. 'Nice, love the fifties vibe, but you could show a bit more cleavage.'

Sabrina raised a brow.

'You did ask,' her sister said.

'No, actually I didn't.'

'Well, you should. Have you any idea how many people read my fashion blog? I am considered a fashion guru.'

'And what do you think Dad is going to consider about *that*?'

Sabrina angled a nod in the direction of the micro miniskirt her sister was wearing in neon green.

'He won't see it,' Chloe said with a grin as she rolled over and pulled herself into a sitting position, her long legs tucked under her.

It was then Sabrina saw what her sister was wearing on top.

Chloe gave another million-voltage smile and held her arms wide to proudly show off the T-shirt. Sabrina had seen identical ones in the tourist shops in the capital of Vela Main, where the iconic image was reproduced on everything from tea towels to mugs. It was of the Venetian Prince who had fought for, and gained, independence for Vela.

'You like? I'm showing my hands-across-the-border solidarity. They say his eyes follow you round the room.'

'They do,' Sabrina said shortly. She had seen the original on the wall of the great hall in the royal palace.

'Don't you think their Pirate Prince looks like the bad brother? I can't see how anyone could have thought he was a bastard,' Chloe added, pulling the fabric outwards to look at the face of the Venetian Prince famous for being the man who had fought dirty to secure Vela Main's independence from Venice. That, and his career as a successful pirate.

It was Luis who had pointed out the similarity during a day trip her family had made the previous year to take lunch with the royal family at Vela Main.

'His eyes really do follow you around the room,' she

had said, staring at the original of the much-reproduced image.

'Sebastian has the same trick,' Luis had said.

'He was very handsome. Him,' she'd added, pointing at the portrait and adding hastily, 'Not your brother.'

Luis had laughed at her embarrassment. 'You might change your mind when you two finally meet. I'd like to say Seb got the looks and I got the brains, but...'

'I think you're very smart, modest and good-looking.'

Whenever doubts had crept in Sabrina had reminded herself that Luis couldn't have been more unlike his hateful brother if he'd tried.

They were day and night, Sebastian definitely being night, even though his eyes had made her think of the brightest, most blindingly blue summer sky when he'd bent his head and fitted his cool, firm lips to hers.

She felt the guilty heat rise through her body as she reminded herself that she *could* have stopped it from happening!

Belatedly aware that Chloe was staring at her, she shook her head.

'A bit,' she conceded before changing the subject. 'God, you look like an advert for something healthy... or toothpaste?'

'And you, sweetie, look like you were doorstepped by the national media.' She held out her arms. 'Hug?'

'Yes, please.'

Sisterly hug exchanged, they sat down on the window seat side by side.

'I'm quite jealous of the number of hits you got... did you watch it?'

Sabrina did not pretend not to understand; she had heard she had gone viral. 'No, I was there.'

'Don't look so gloomy. I know many women who

would pay to get chucked into the back seat by Sebastian Zorzi, and you were wearing nice undies.'

Sabrina's eyes widened. 'You couldn't…?'

Chloe chuckled at the shocked reaction. 'No, just a lot of leg.' Her expression sobered. 'Seriously, though…?'

Sabrina angled an enquiring look at her sister's face.

The grin re-emerged. 'He is seriously gorgeous! How about a double wedding? I'm up for it if you are!'

'What, and share my day in the spotlight?' Sabrina said, struggling to reply in kind because the image of her sister, dressed in white, standing beside a tall, lean, handsome figure made her feel a little queasy.

'Because we all know how much you love that.' Chloe's smile vanished. 'Brina, are you all right? I'm just trying to lighten the mood, you know. Are you really going to do it?'

'Do what?'

'Go through with this crazy medieval marriage of convenience? You can't let yourself be used this way, Brina. It's so wrong.'

'I don't have a choice.'

'There is always a choice, Brina.'

Sabrina shook her head and veiled her eyes with her lashes. It was true, but now the time was here she wished she believed it. 'I want to marry Luis. He's a nice guy.'

Chloe's expression grew serious as she took her sister's hands in hers and said gravely, 'Don't you think you deserve better than *nice*? A husband who thinks you are more important than anything?'

After a shocked moment Sabrina brought her lashes down in a protective sweep as she swallowed the emotional lump in her throat. Chloe had voiced the thoughts she didn't dare even allow herself to think.

'Since when did you become a paid-up member of the soppy romantic club?'

Chloe's smile was back as she jumped to her feet. 'I hide it well. So how about I do wear this tonight?' She moved her hand down the tiny skirt she wore. 'And flirt with the sexy Sebastian?'

Sabrina struggled to respond to her sister's teasing smile, managing some sickly approximation of an answering smile despite the tight feeling of rejection in her stomach.

'Chloe, be careful. Sebastian Zorzi, he isn't the sort of man you play with.'

She thought of eyes so blue they took your breath away and felt a little shiver trace a sinuous path down her spine as the memory surfaced, both terrifying and seductive. She didn't want Chloe to be exposed to the danger he represented.

Or maybe you don't want her to be kissed.

'He's dangerous.'

Chloe laughed. 'He sounds better and better. Now how about a glass of wine to get us in the mood, or to at least prepare me for the undoubted cold shower that awaits me when I go to my room? Perhaps when you've sold your body for the good of the country we can get the plumbing fixed?' She grinned and produced a bottle from the capacious handbag she had dumped by the door. 'Glasses?'

CHAPTER THREE

HER MOTHER ENTERED her bedroom with dramatic abrupt-
ness just as Sabrina was fitting the last hair in the smooth
twist she had wound her hair into.

'There has been a disaster with the meal. Don't ask!'

Sabrina didn't but the harassed Duchess told her anyway. 'I found out an hour ago that the Queen is gluten
and lactose intolerant. Half the menu had to be revised.
The chef is not happy.'

'I'm sure it will be fine,' Sabrina soothed, getting to
her feet. Focusing on her mother's panic made it somehow easier to deal with her own nerves. 'Just breathe,
Mum.' She laid a hand on her parent's arm.

The Duchess took a deep breath. 'Yes, I'm sure
you're right, but I'm running terribly late. I haven't
even started getting ready, not that it really matters.
The Queen—' she lowered her voice and glanced over
her shoulder, as though someone might be listening,
before adding in a note of mingled envy and despair
'—always makes me feel inadequate. I swear the
woman gets younger every year!'

'Mum, you always look lovely!' Sabrina protested.

Her mother smiled. 'You're a good girl, Brina. And
you're right, of course, at my age it's silly to worry about
what I look like.'

'I didn't say that,' Sabrina protested. 'There's plenty of time for you to go and get ready.'

'I can't. I promised Walter that I'd run through the final details with him and speak to the staff.'

'Leave it to me,' Sabrina said, pretty sure she would regret the offer. The major-domo, Walter, always made her feel as though she were ten again and he'd just caught her trying to glue together a piece of porcelain she had broken. 'You go and get ready.'

'Really?'

Sabrina nodded.

The Duchess gave her daughter a gentle hug. 'You're an angel. I really don't know what I'll do without you when you're married.'

'Pretty much what you've been doing for the past seven years while I've been living in London, except from now on I'll be closer.

'Of course. You're such a sensible girl. You've never given us a moment's worry, unlike your sister! Speaking of Chloe, I'm going to check what she's wearing.' Reaching the door, she stopped and turned back. 'You look very beautiful tonight.'

Sabrina grinned and smoothed the full skirt of the calf-length fifties-style pale blue silk dress she wore. 'Oh, this old thing?'

'And you're wearing your grandmother's pearls,' the Duchess said, an emotional crack in her voice, as Sabrina touched the string of antique pearls wound around her slender neck. 'You do know we are both very proud of you, don't you? I wish there was another way. That you could—'

'Nobody is forcing me to do anything. Luis is a lovely guy and I plan on being very happy.' She took her mother by the shoulders and propelled her out of the door. It was only when the door had closed again that her forced smile faded. Happiness, she reminded herself, was not a right; in her case it was more a hope.

Sabrina didn't search out the major domo; she knew he'd find her. She relayed her mother's concerns, being careful not to tread on Walter's toes. He responded with his habitual air of statuesque calm to her queries. It was at his suggestion she had a few words with the staff, mainly to thank them for their efforts in hosting the royal party at such short notice.

Then, with Walter, she checked out the table setting in the formal dining room. It was a room they rarely used as a family, but tonight the table groaned with silver and crystal, and happily the candlelight hid a multitude of sins—including the massive crack in the ceiling, which the engineer's report had ominously referred to as significant.

There was, it seemed, only one decision for her to make.

'Her Grace had not decided if we should serve the aperitifs in here, or the small salon?'

It was a courtesy, she knew, because Sabrina had already seen the scene set in the salon as she'd walked past, but she happily maintained the illusion that it was her decision and responded to the courtesy enquiry gravely. 'I think, the small salon.'

The major-domo tipped his head in stately approval of her response. 'I will see to it. If there is nothing else…?'

'Nothing, thank you, Walter.' About to follow him from the room herself, Sabrina paused and turned back. She walked across to the row of French doors that lined one wall and she began to open them up. The last one stubbornly refused to budge, causing her to curse softly. She aimed an irritated kick at it with one narrow, elegantly shod foot, before she paused to get her breath.

The same cool draught of mountain air that Sebastian felt on his face as he reached the open doorway made the full skirt of Sabrina's dress billow around her slender legs. He watched as, eyes closed, long lashes fanning darkly against her smooth cheeks, eyes squeezed closed, she let out a long sibilant sigh through parted pink lips as she turned her face into the breeze, making no attempt to tame the fabric as it lifted and fluttered some more.

The tilt of her chin and the elegant placement of her arms made him think of a ballet dancer. An idea that was reinforced as her head fell back revealing the long, lovely line of her neck and throat and the angles of her collarbones. Though high to the throat, at the back the bodice of the dress she wore was cut into a deep vee that exposed a half-moon-shaped mole on the crest of one delicate shoulder blade.

Sebastian felt the heat rise through him and forgot to breathe, forgot *how* to breathe as the graceful image burned deep into his brain. Hunger tightened its grip, a primal pleasure/pain presence low in his belly and all points south. There were so many warning bells ringing in his head that he was deaf to everything but the heavy thud of his heart, the ache in his body and the whisper of sound as the fabric brushed against her legs.

Then she opened her eyes and gave a tiny sigh. The sound snapped the sensual spell that had held him transfixed, leaving behind something that he refused to recognise as tenderness. That sigh had sounded so damn *wistful*.

She remained oblivious to his presence as he crossed

the room. She had both hands braced against the door frame and was pushing against the stubborn door, when he placed a hand above her head on the door jamb.

The door gave with a shudder.

'Thank you.' Sabrina turned, the corners of her soft mouth lifted in a smile of gratitude, which melded into one of dismay as she saw that it was him.

Sabrina stepped back so quickly that she almost lost her balance. The impact of his physical proximity acted like a live current, her quivering stomach vanished into a bottomless black hole and it took every ounce of her willpower to stop herself backing through the open door, which would have been impossible anyway because her limbs were paralyzed with shock. *They call it lust, Brina.*

Ignoring the mocking voice in her head, she lifted her softly rounded chin to a warily aggressive angle and directed a cool look up at the tall figure of the Zorzi black sheep. Sebastian just stood there in his formal black tie and tux, looking as if he had just stepped off a glossy Hollywood set.

'You're too early!' Panic made her voice sharp.

'I could hardly wait to sample the well-known hospitality of East Vela,' he countered sardonically as his heavy-lidded stare travelled from the top of her glossy head to her heels and back. Sabrina fingered the pearls at her throat, trying desperately to ignore how his assessing and overtly sensual gaze made her whole body tingle.

The nervous action drew his stare to her throat, where a blue-veined pulse pushed against the pale skin.

'You startled me. I thought you were Walter.'

So the smile was for Walter. 'You look…good.'

No smile came with the compliment, which was delivered in an expressionless voice.

'So, should I?'

'What?'

'Go away and come back.'

Sabrina flushed and moved her head slightly to look past his shoulder willing someone, anyone, to appear.

They didn't.

'If you were expecting Luis he's waiting on an important call.'

She firmed her shoulders and reminded herself that being pleasant to people she didn't like was part of her future job. She could not allow personal feelings to enter into it. 'No, of course not. You just took me by surprise and this is a bit…awkward.'

'Why?'

She tightened her lips and glared at him. 'I have no pleasant memories of our last encounter.'

'I can think of one,' he teased, looking at her mouth.

The longer their glances held, the thicker the atmosphere in the air became. Sabrina was the first to look away, fixing her eyes on a point over his shoulder as she fiddled with the pearls. 'I had assumed you were drunk but I can see now that you're always…' Her words faded as the vivid memory resurfaced. His breath the other day had not actually tasted of booze, just mint and… No, she was not going to go there!

'Irresistible?'

Before she could react to the suggestion the antique string of pearls she was playing with snapped.

Sabrina immediately fell to her knees, trying to grab the pearls, which were bouncing across the polished wooden floor in all directions. 'Oh, no! No, no, no.'

'Relax, they're not the crown jewels…' He stopped, his teasing look vanishing from his face as she lifted her head and he saw that she was close to tears.

'Just go away!' she hissed. 'I don't give a damn about the crown jewels. They were my grandmother's pearls.'

With a frown he dropped down, squatting on his heels beside her. He saw the little tremors that shook her shoulders and felt something twist hard in his chest. He did his best to ignore it, telling himself it was either indigestion or the threat of tears that had caused it. He'd never liked seeing women crying.

'She left them to me. She always wore them and now they're ruined! *Everything* is ruined…' Dignity forgotten, on all fours now, she stretched to retrieve a pearl that had slipped under a chair, but as her finger touched it it bounced away. 'I can't do this! It's so, so… No, I just can't!'

'What we need is a system. An inch-by-inch search. What do they call it—a fingertip search?'

The image that drifted into her head involved his fingertips moving very slowly, but the surface they were exploring, the secret crevices they were discovering, had nothing to do with the wooden floor! What was happening to her?

'You count and I'll retrieve.'

She struggled to drag her thoughts back to the present. The process felt like swimming through warm honey. There was a horrible temptation to taste it.

'That really isn't necessary,' she managed finally, her voice carrying nowhere near the level of conviction she was hoping for. 'I'm really not that sentimental.'

He had already lifted the heavy starched linen tablecloth; at her comment he glanced back over his shoulder. 'Yes, you are, which is fine. Make yourself useful and hold this up. There are some under here.'

After a pause she did as he requested and lifted the heavy starched linen cloth while he reached under. A moment later several more pearls were dropped into her open hand.

She glanced at him from under her lashes. His dark hair was ruffled and there was a dusty smudge on the dark lapel of his jacket. Without thinking she reached out to brush it away. 'You don't have to do this, you know.'

'I know.'

She had never seen anything as blue as his eyes; they were compellingly hypnotic. She fought a short internal battle and dropped her hand away, escaping the full impact of his eyes by looking up through the mesh of her lashes. 'Well, thank you, I think that's all of them,' she said at last, closing her hand that was now full of the smooth pearls.

Sebastian rose to his feet before her and reached out a hand. After a pause Sabrina took it and allowed him to pull her to her feet. Her stomach made an unscheduled dive as her quivering nostrils picked up the scent of his warm body, the clean fragrance, the *maleness*.

He immediately released her hand but she could still feel the warmth of his fingers as she rubbed her hand along her silk-covered thigh. The stab of sexual desire that pierced her was so tangible it seemed to her guilty mind that it echoed off the walls like an accusation.

'I've been meaning to get them restrung for ages.' She began to babble. What was he trying to do to her? Nothing, came the depressing and shaming answer, he didn't have to do a thing.

'Lady Sabrina?'

She responded with relief to the sound of her name and the familiar respectful voice. 'Yes, Walter?' she said, moving towards the door where the major-domo stood.

'I just wanted to let you know that the Duke and Duchess are in the small salon.' He turned towards Sebastian and bent forward at the waist. 'Sir, I believe that the royal party will be joining them there directly.'

'I'll be right there, Walter,' Sabrina said, shifting the pearls from one slightly sticky hand to the other.

'May I help?'

'These are my—'

'The late Duchess's pearls.' The major-domo gave one of his rare smiles and held out a hand. 'I never saw her without them,' he added when Sabrina looked reluctant. 'They will be safe with me.'

Sabrina acknowledged the reassurance with a smile and tipped the pearls into his hand. 'Thank you.' She stood there, hopefully not looking as awkward as she felt as she turned back to Sebastian, who had watched the interchange in silence. Not quite meeting his eyes—some might call it cowardly but she called it sensible—she gestured towards the door. 'I'll show you the way, shall I?' Without waiting to see if he accepted the invitation, she left the room, not caring if she gave the impression of running away. Any woman with an ounce of common sense would run in the opposite direction when they saw Sebastian Zorzi, though she doubted there were many who did. Luckily she had never been one of the number who were drawn to danger, even when it wore a suit as well as he did. He probably looked even better without the suit!

Face flushed with shame, she speeded up, but she had only gone a few yards before he fell into step beside her.

'I never met your grandmother. But I've heard a lot about her. She sounds like quite a character.'

'She always said exactly what she thought.' And her outspoken grandparent had thought that the plan to marry her granddaughter off to seal the reunification deal was an appalling plan and she had said so, often. 'Chloe is very like her. Not in looks obviously.' Her grandmother had been tiny and delicate while her sister would not have looked out of place in an Olympic rowing team.

'But not you?'

'Gran was a rebel,' Sabrina said, aware of the emotional ache in her throat but not of the wistful quality to her observation as she thought of the old lady who had been such a big part of her early years. 'So, no, we are not alike. I'm a *good* girl, remember?' she said, forgetting her intention not to look at him and angling a resentful look up at his dark, lean, *insanely* handsome face.

Sebastian intercepted the glare and held her eyes as he raised a dark sardonic brow before allowing his stare to sink to her mouth, heat sparking in his heavy-lidded eyes as they moved across the full soft curves. 'Not always,' he purred throatily.

She looked away quickly, feeling the heat climb to her cheeks as the volume of the background hum of sexual awareness that she had been successfully dealing with up until now became a deafening clamour.

'We all make mistakes. I think the trick is in not repeating them,' she said. Two could play the innuendo game! 'Here we are,' she added, as a young maid carrying a tray bobbed a little curtsy. The younger woman's wide appreciative eyes stayed firmly on Sebastian as she almost bumped into the full suit of armour that was positioned beside the door they had reached before walking through, head down now to hide her burning cheeks.

Sabrina angled a sideways look at Sebastian, who didn't even seem to have noticed. Presumably, she thought bitterly, he was used to women falling over when they saw him.

Glass houses, Brina?

Ignoring the sly contribution of the voice in her head, she walked ahead of him into the room, where her parents greeted her with an exchange of relieved looks before glaring at Chloe, who sat twirling an olive on a stick in her drink.

'I only said she *might* have had second thoughts,' her sister defended, opening her eyes innocently wide. Her eyes widened further, only not so innocently this time, as Sebastian appeared behind her sister.

Her father, his hand extended, immediately moved to greet the younger man, assuring him how delighted they were that he was able to join them.

'And I must tell you how grateful we were that you were able to extract Sabrina here from that unpleasant situation earlier in the week.'

'Oh, for heaven's sake, Dad, you make it sound as though he led a black ops rescue mission. He merely gave me a lift in his car!'

Her horrified parents turned, twin expressions of embarrassed disapproval on both their faces.

'Sabrina!'

Wishing she had kept her mouth shut but equally unable to back down, she shrugged. 'Well, it's true. I could have got a taxi and there would have been less fuss.' And no guilty secrets.

'What has come over you, Sabrina?' her mother asked, regarding her elder daughter with horror. 'I apologise, Sebastian, for—'

'No need at all. Sabrina is right—it was no bother. I was in the area.'

'You mean you were falling out of a nightclub!'

That's the way to go, Brina, because the hole you had dug was not deep enough.

'Oh, the new one that everyone is talking about?
Is it really as gloriously debauched as everyone said,
and did Laura really dance topless on the table?' Chloe
asked, winking at Sabrina as she drew the parental fire
onto her own head. But before she got a response to
any of her questions Luis entered the room ahead of
his parents.

Sabrina, her eyes lowered, performed a curtsy when
her turn came.

The Queen, enveloped in a cloud of perfume, put a
hand under her chin and while Sabrina fought the urge
to snatch it away she turned her chin to the light.

'She is so pretty. Isn't she pretty, Ricard?'

She appealed to her husband who, after raising a
brow at the presence of his younger son, was accepting the glass of champagne that had been offered him.

'Lovely cheekbones.'

'Delightful,' the King responded, not looking at Sabrina or her cheekbones or, to her relief, her child-bear-
ing hips, which were probably the only attribute in his
future daughter-in-law that interested him, but staring
at the glass of champagne he held.

He wasn't holding it for long. The Queen released
Sabrina and promptly removed it from his hand.

'Doctor's orders,' she explained, and handed him an
orange-juice-filled flute.

Aware that Luis had come to stand beside her, Sabrina turned with a smile.

'Did you have a good journey?' she asked, hearing
the fake bright note in her voice. If she couldn't think
of something to say to him now, what would it be like
in twenty years' time? She let her eyes drift to where
Sebastian stood talking to her sister, knowing there was

no logic to it but blaming him for the horrid sinking feeling in the pit of her stomach anyway.

'Pretty good considering.'

Chloe had moved away but she could still hear her sister's laughter as Sebastian, who followed her, spoke in a low rumble, his words inaudible.

'And did your call go well, Luis?'

'Call?' Luis repeated, his expression suddenly guarded, even, weirdly, *suspicious*...

'Your brother said that you were waiting on an important call.'

Luis seemed to relax a little and Sabrina decided she had misread his veiled expression. 'Oh, yes, sure, it was not really important. Sebastian must have got the wrong idea.'

When five minutes later dinner was announced the small gathering left the room. Protocol demanded that the King, with the Duchess on his arm, led the party, followed by the Queen and the Duke. Before Luis could take her own arm and fall into place behind them, Chloe slid between them, taking Luis's arm.

'Your bad brother has been telling me some things—' she flung a laughing glance over her shoulder '—and I really don't know if they're true. Tell me, how do you know if he's lying?'

'I'm hurt at the accusation I would ever tell an untruth,' Sebastian protested as Chloe led his brother away.

Watching the little interchange Sabrina felt a stab of something that resembled jealousy, enough to increase the level of conflict swirling in her head by several uncomfortable, confusing notches.

'Shall we?'

Looking from the arm presented to her to his face,

she gave a quick nod and placed her hand lightly on it. While the couples ahead made light conversation, in contrast they walked in silence down the hallway until they reached the dining-room doorway.

'What is it?' Sebastian asked, refusing to acknowledge the stab of sympathy as she stood there, her slim body in an attitude that made him think of a scared animal trying to work up the courage to move out of the headlights. Or in Sabrina's case, he supposed, to step into the spotlight.

'Nothing,' she said, forcing the word through pale lips. 'Just…just give me a minute, would you?'

The sympathy he'd held in check turned into anger as he watched her.

'Is it worth it?'

The harsh scorn in his voice forced her gaze upwards. She felt her anger rise, hot and resentful. 'Financial stability, a reduction in the unemployment rate, an education system that is fit for purpose…funding for—' She took a deep breath, her expression hard with contempt when she finished. 'Is that worth me marrying a man I respect and like? Yes, I think so.' She let go of his arm and, chin up, shoulders firm, she walked in ahead of him.

Sebastian watched her queenly progress and felt a stab of something that he refused to recognise as respect.

CHAPTER FOUR

Taking her own seat, Sabrina watched as Chloe, already seated, said something to make the normally severe guest of honour laugh. Sabrina felt a stab of envy for the social ease that came so naturally to her sister, who tonight looked particularly stunning in a slim-fitting flame-red shift. Sabrina could work the room with the best of them when required, but it had been a learnt process. With Chloe it came naturally.

As the waiting staff began to circulate the table Sabrina struggled to force her mind back to Luis, seated to her right, responding with an ambiguous nod because she didn't have a clue as to what he'd just said before. Her eyes were drawn across the table where Chloe was now talking to Sebastian.

Then, as a waiter moved between them, Sebastian's gaze shifted. Caught staring, Sabrina looked away quickly and grabbed Luis's hand.

She ignored the mortifying fact that Luis's first instinct was to pull away and she couldn't ignore the look of alarm in his eyes when she'd laughed quite inanely, as though he'd just said something desperately amusing.

'Sabrina dear,' her mother said. 'They are trying to serve the soup. If you must hold hands...'

Everyone looked and Sabrina let go of Luis's hand,

keeping the blush at bay by sheer force of will. Rather to her surprise he kept hold of it. He actually turned it over, then she realised what he was looking at.

She should either have put on some make-up to cover the bruises on the inside of her forearm or worn long sleeves.

'How did that happen?' Luis said, directing a concerned frown at the darkening patches either side of her arm.

'I bruise easily,' she said quickly, putting her hand across her middle.

'Since when?' Chloe asked.

'Let me see that, Sabrina.'

'It's fine, Mum, it probably happened when I was jostled by the press.'

'Those animals!' her protective father rumbled, his face dark with anger as he surged awkwardly to his feet.

'Arnica,' her mother said, her eyes on her husband, who after a moment subsided in his seat. 'It really helps bruising. I wonder if we have any...'

'I'm fine!' Sabrina said, her smile strained. 'Just fine, it's nothing and—' She took a deep breath and addressed the rest of her comment directly to Sebastian. 'I'd like to put what happened behind me, to forget about it and move on.'

A three-year-old could have read the coded message but she found it frustratingly impossible to tell from his expression if *he* had understood.

It was the King, who was seated at the head of the table, who picked up her theme. 'We'd *all* like to move on,' he pronounced suddenly.

It was rare that he and his father were on the same page but on this occasion moving on seemed an excellent idea and one Sebastian realised he needed to put into action at the first possible opportunity.

He felt as if a protective layer had been stripped from his skin. It wasn't just what he felt, it was how *much* he felt.

He'd made the connection between those finger marks on Sabrina's arm and his rough and ready extraction method the moment Luis had drawn everyone's attention to them. Knowing he was responsible had shaken loose this painful cascade of emotions he could not identify, emotions he had never come close to feeling in his life before. The depth of the self-loathing he felt was visceral in its intensity.

Having waited until he had everyone's attention, the King continued, in a deeply disgruntled tone. 'Though there seems little chance of that when we have that damned book to look forward to. If the legal team had not been persuaded by a *certain someone*.' The direction of his poisonous glare left little doubt who the *someone* in question was.

The only person who didn't look uncomfortable was the target of the King's venom.

Sebastian's broad shoulders lifted in the slightest of shrugs, the cool in his eyes as icy as his father's barely concealed antagonism was hot.

'I was asked for my opinion and I gave it, Father,' Sebastian responded calmly. 'I have no idea if it influenced the advice you were given, but I thought and I still do think that though a gagging injunction might have prevented the book being published in the UK, it would have been nothing more than a delay. And with people being able to access the details and the book online it would simply have been good publicity for the author.'

'Why *did* the lawyers ask you?' Chloe, who had been listening with curiosity to the interchange, asked.

The King gave a laugh and, ignoring his wife's speaking look, nodded to have his wine glass filled. 'Good question, young lady.'

'It was a field that I worked in for a while.'

'You're a lawyer? Why didn't I know that?' Chloe asked the table in general. 'I thought I'd read everything there was to know about you.'

Sabrina, who had felt the tension that had been building in Luis while his brother and father faced off, was less surprised than the others when he replied to Chloe's question.

'You tend to read about my little brother falling out of nightclubs, Chloe, but before he became the playboy of the western world he graduated top of his class at Harvard law and worked for the best legal firm in New York. He was even offered a partnership.'

Glancing towards Sebastian, Sabrina glimpsed an expression that on anyone else she would have labelled embarrassment.

The King, looking annoyed at the interruption, took over the story. 'But he chose to risk everything and—'

'I'm not really a team-player, Father,' Sebastian interrupted.

'You're a gambler!' his father condemned.

'Father!' Luis protested.

'It's all right, Luis, stock speculators are frequently called worse.'

'Gamblers lose money, Seb, you don't. And,' Luis added, addressing his remark to the rest of the table, 'Sebastian does pro bono work for at least one charity that helps...'

His heated defence came to a stumbling halt when

the King, whose normally florid colouring had taken on an alarming purplish hue, cleared his throat loudly and drawled contemptuously, 'I'm sure we feel honoured to have a financial genius and altruist in our family.'

The Queen reached out and laid her hand over her husband's. 'Not the time, Ricard,' she murmured softly.

The effort to respond to her warning glance deepened the unhealthy ruddiness another couple of shades before the table was engulfed in a painfully awkward silence, broken after a few uncomfortable moments by the Duchess.

'Sabrina, I thought you were wearing your grandmother's pearls earlier?'

Sabrina shook her head as the knot of anger in her chest grew. She struggled, and failed, to dampen the tide of righteous fury that was making her head spin. She took a deep breath and exhaled it slowly through flared nostrils. King Ricard, in her opinion, was a poor excuse for a parent—he was in fact a *bully*!

'A slight mishap,' she managed finally, unable to stop her glance flickering towards Sebastian. There had been no *mishap* involved in the King's attempt to belittle his son. Sebastian might not need looking after now, but he didn't deserve—*nobody* deserved—his parent trying to humiliate him in public, and there was no doubt that that was what the King had been trying to do.

It hadn't worked but she could imagine a time in the past that it had, probably when Sebastian had been young. Oh, but she *hated* bullies! An image of Sebastian as a child floated into her head.

Had Luis been defending him then, too?

There was warmth in her eyes as she flashed her future husband a smile. She had really admired the way he had defended his brother and if she was honest she'd been surprised by it. She felt a little ashamed that she'd had such low expectations of him.

'What happened to the pearls, Sabrina?' her mother pushed for details. 'You haven't lost them?'

'Of course not, they need restringing.' She closed her mouth, not intending to say anything but her wretched imagination had taken hold and that image in her head just wouldn't go away. Two brothers united in fear of their father, and she couldn't stop herself. 'You must be really proud...'

During the seconds it took the King to realise she was talking to him, Sabrina felt her mother's alarm and deliberately didn't look her way.

'Proud of your sons,' she clarified with another brilliant smile that hid not just her anger but the fact that she wished she had not started this. It wasn't as if Sebastian weren't big and beautiful enough to look after himself.

He hadn't always been big but that he'd always been beautiful was a given. As hard as it might be to imagine now, she could see the boy he had been without the armour he possessed now taking what amounted to mental abuse from his father, who somehow and unfairly blamed him for his mother's infidelities. There was no excuse in Sabrina's mind.

'And what they have achieved.'

Despite you, she thought, meeting his icy glare and, realising that if she let him think he could intimidate her she'd set the pattern for the next years of her life, she didn't look away. 'They are a credit to you,' she said, daring him to deny it.

After a pause during which it felt as if the entire table held their collective breath, though that might have only been her because she had realised that in challenging the King she might just have caused a diplomatic incident, the King nodded his head and grunted.

So no diplomatic incident, just a very, *very* unfriendly look… It could have been worse, though maybe not much.

'My mother,' the Duchess said, her voice bright. 'My mother always wore those pearls. They were her signature. Really, Sabrina, you should have taken more care. Are you *sure* you didn't lose any?'

By the time the subject of the pearls had been exhausted the King's colour had returned to normal and the rest of the meal passed without incident, though the King quite pointedly did not address his younger son. Not that the silent treatment seemed to bother the object of his disapproval.

The meal over, it seemed like an age to Sabrina before the King rose and gestured to Luis. 'A word,' he instructed, before nodding to his hosts and sweeping out, leaving the Queen behind.

As he was about to leave Luis leaned in. 'I wonder if you'd take a walk in the rose garden with me later, Sabrina?'

So I can sign away the rest of my life and become an invisible helpmate and mother of your children—why not? Then she felt guilty because Luis looked as miserable and tense as she felt.

'That would be lovely,' she said politely.

This is not about you, Brina. This is about more important things like the future, schools, people's jobs.

And it could work. They could skip the entire 'falling out of love' part so often involved in marriage by never being in love to begin with.

Her father's voice broke into her introspection.

'Shall we leave the ladies, Sebastian? I have an excellent brandy in my study.'

Sabrina was surprised; her father's study was his sanctuary. She couldn't recall him inviting anyone into it. He must have taken a liking to the black sheep, or more likely he was trying to compensate for the way Sebastian's father had treated him. Perhaps like her he had noticed how quiet Sebastian had been for the remainder of the meal.

The tension that hummed inside Sebastian as he left the room behind the Duke had nothing to do with his father's open hostility but the fact that Sabrina had stood up to the King, defending both him and Luis.

Nobody had *ever* done that, and in doing so she had probably made herself a target. His jaw clenched. Didn't she see that men like his father responded to flattery, not a challenge to their authority? Chloe knew that, the Duchess knew that, yet Sabrina had just stuck out her chin. Did she think he needed a champion? Did she think he couldn't look after himself?

He'd seen her shaking, whether from anger or fear he'd been unable to tell, but she'd been pretty damned magnificent. An idiot, but a beautiful, brave idiot!

Sabrina went to get herself a wrap before she ventured out into the gardens. She had not reached the rose garden when Luis appeared on the path ahead.

'I didn't actually find the rose gardens. I got a bit lost.'

'That's fine, it's over that way, beyond the tennis courts, but we really don't have to go that far. Here is fine, unless you are really that interested in the roses? Or am I making an assumption?'

Luis lowered his gaze from her direct look. 'No, you're not,' he admitted, dragging a hand through his fairish hair. He had inherited his mother's colouring.

She tried to visualise him in ten, twenty years' time and found she couldn't, though oddly she could see Sebastian. Perhaps a few more lines around his eyes, a little more cynicism in their depths, maybe a strand of grey or two, but his incredible bone structure virtually guaranteed that he would look essentially the same.

You are about to be proposed to by one brother and you're thinking about the other, Sabrina.

'We've never…' She stopped, realising she couldn't ask him to kiss her so she could forget being kissed by his brother. 'Can I ask you to do something for me?'

She watched a look of caution drift across his face.

'Don't worry, I'm not going to ask you to say you love me.' His flush suggested she had correctly interpreted his alarm, but this wasn't about love. She didn't love either of the Zorzi brothers.

With Sebastian it was simply sex, or it would be, and with Luis it was respect. Respect lasted longer and was, she told herself, a much sounder basis for marriage.

'Sorry, I've never been proposed to before and I'm— Oh, no—look you don't have to—' She stopped because Luis had already dropped to his knees.

'Will you do me the honour of—?'

'For God's sake, yes—get up, please! Sorry, I—' On his feet, Luis held out a ring in a velvet-lined box. The diamond looked bigger than most continents as it flashed in the moonlight. 'Wow, how…very…large. I'm—' She stopped as the ring was slid onto her finger. 'I suppose as it's already there I should say…well… I suppose…yes.'

Not exactly a ringing endorsement but her husband-to-be looked satisfied, or that might have been relief that it was all over. 'That's great. We can make this work, can't we, Sabrina?'

She met his earnest gaze, noticed the beads of moisture along his upper lip. 'Everyone needs to work at marriage.'

'That's true,' he said, acting as though her clenched response were actually wisdom and not desperation. 'Would you like to come with me while I tell my father?'

'I'll wait here.' She caught his arm as he turned to go. 'Aren't you forgetting something?'

He looked bemused.

'A kiss?' She had been half joking but Luis's expression became serious.

'Of course.' He took her shoulders and leaned in.

Sabrina closed her eyes and held her breath. The brush of his lips across her mouth hardly constituted a kiss. She opened her eyes and endured an awkward pause.

'We really should go and tell the families together, present a united front.'

'You go ahead. I'll... I'll just take a moment.' A moment to appreciate that she was marrying a man whose kiss had had absolutely no effect on her—unlike the response a kiss from his brother had drawn. She expelled a long sigh, her glance drifting to the ring on her finger.

Her dark eyes flickered wide as the full implication of its presence there sank in, or rather seeped out from the pit of her stomach until her entire body was ice cold.

Now it was just a matter of waiting for someone to realise how not up to the task she was.

She stood there breathing through the moment of sheer panic, willing calmness to flow through her body.

Then her chin lifted. 'Time to step up, Sabrina.'

* * *

'For a woman who is about to live every little girl's dream, you don't sound very happy.'

He was here, of *course* he was here. She must have done something very bad in a previous life and she was paying for it now.

Heart thudding heavily, she turned around just as Sebastian appeared, a dark shadow surrounded by the darker shadow of the undergrowth.

'Happiness is not a right and I am not a little girl.'

He stopped being shadow and stepped forward into the light.

At some point since he'd left the table he had discarded his jacket, his unfastened tie hung around his neck and the top three buttons of his shirt were open. She could see the faint shadow of dark chest hair and it made her insides quiver.

Stop, she told herself firmly. There was no point wanting something you couldn't have. And she should be glad of it; he'd have used her as he used all women, except, *maybe she wanted to be used*?

Unwilling to deal with the sight of him standing there, the sheer physicality of his presence, she took refuge in spitting anger.

'How long have you been standing there?' If he had seen the awful, miserable proposal she would die.

'Relax,' he drawled. 'It's not like I saw you making mad, passionate love in the shrubbery.' His eyes drifted over her head to the stone wall with clematis clinging to it. 'Or up against the wall.'

The suggestive rasp in his voice sent a deep shudder through Sabrina's body. 'How *dare* you spy on me?' she squeaked, making the mistake of telling herself she wouldn't think about the wall. So obviously that was all she could think of…being pressed up against it, his hands on her body, on her skin.

'Spy? I almost drifted off. How was I to know my brother would not bother to go more than two steps from the back door to propose?' The indents between his eyebrows deepened as his dark brows drew together in a straight line above his heavy-lidded eyes. 'If that actually constituted a proposal!'

His flaying scorn at least threw cold water on the fantasy images in her head.

'Your brother is worth ten of you!'

'Oh, more, angel, much, *much* more.'

'And just because he treats me with some respect and doesn't grope me.'

'If memory serves, you groped me right back.'

She compressed her lips. 'Go to hell!'

'Language…'

'What can I say? I was taught by nuns.'

'They must be very proud of how you've turned out. Actually, hell is a bit warm for me at this time of year. I thought Paris, you know what they say, Paris in the springtime…though it's bit late for that.'

His contemptuous attitude stung. 'I wouldn't expect you to understand the concept of duty. I wouldn't expect you to understand anything except your own selfish—' Breathing hard, she broke off. 'I have no idea why I'm even trying. Have you *ever* in your life done anything that wasn't selfish?'

'My lifestyle is not the issue. It's the thought of yours that is scaring you. You can see the rest of your life stretching out in front of you and you don't like it. This is your choice, *cara*, so don't blame me!'

Her chin went up and she took a step towards him. 'My life will be a hell of a lot more fulfilling than yours, unless of course you count chasing anything in a skirt fulfilling. And I will have a husband I can respect!'

He clenched his jaw, the tension causing a quiver of muscles under the surface of his skin as he held his breath until the stab of pain that felt like a dull blade sliding between his ribs became a manageable dull ache.

Acknowledging it as jealousy would take him to a place he didn't want to go, so instead he turned his frustration on the woman standing there.

'And Luis is going to *respect* you right back. Every girl's dream, I suppose, but then a crown *is* worth a few compromises.' Even as he tossed the accusation at her he recognised the unfairness of it. He was probably one of the few people in a position to understand how trapped she was. 'I pity you.'

She clenched her teeth. 'Don't you *dare* feel sorry for me!' she blazed up at him, her dark eyes flashing.

'I don't feel sorry for you! I feel...' The waste of it, he thought, his eyes sinking to her mouth. All that passion and fire and, despite the alarm bells ringing in his head, he stepped in closer. The moment coincided with the lights from the room that had illuminated the paved area where they stood being switched off.

The moon was behind a cloud and the darkness was total.

Sabrina blinked in the darkness. It was like being wrapped in inky velvet. A thrill of illicit excitement made her stomach clench and raised a rash of goosebumps on her skin.

She made herself think past her thudding heart, recognising the danger. Darkness gave a sense of anonymity; people did things in the darkness that they would not in the light. Except for Sebastian, who did what he liked, when he liked.

What would it feel like, she wondered, to be like that?

'Are you all right?' His deep voice was huskily concerned.

The disembodied question drew a sharp laugh from her. *All right?* So now he was concerned after throwing her into an emotional tsunami, after making her question things that she had never questioned? He had made her want what she could not have *ever*.

Suddenly the fight drained out of her, as she realised she would never be happy, or at least content, until she let go of that tiny grain of irrational hope that the marriage wouldn't really happen, that there would be a last-minute reprieve.

She just had to accept it and not fight, not want more.

'I'm fine. I'm going in. Luis is expecting me to join him.'

'I'll see you in.'

He was closer.

'So suddenly you're the perfect gentleman,' she mocked unsteadily.

Sebastian's eyes had adjusted to the light and her face was a pale blur, her body less distinct. The compulsion to reach for her in the darkness was so strong the effort of fighting it made him quiver like someone with a fever. 'I deserved that, but you deserved a better proposal.'

'Not everyone has your way with words. I suspect the only proposals you have any working knowledge of are of the indecent variety.'

'I may not know much about duty, but you have now agreed to marry my brother so you are totally out of bounds. Even to a total sleaze like me, so you can stop looking at me like that.'

'You don't know how I'm looking at you.'

'I know those big hungry eyes. Just go inside while you still can.'

She shivered, a thrill of excitement shimmering through her body at the message in his dark voice. 'What happens if I don't go inside?'

'You are killing me, you know that, don't you?'

She felt a tide of hot shame wash over her. 'Sorry.'

'Me too.' He heard the swish of her dress as she turned and ran away in the darkness. 'See you at the church, *cara*,' he called softly after her.

CHAPTER FIVE

SEBASTIAN ARRIVED AT the cathedral early. The place was empty but for a group putting the final touches to the flower arrangements that filled the massive space with the overpowering fragrance of orange blossoms.

He hated the pervasive smell but it was better than the alternative—being outside for the orgy of meet-and-greet, hand-wringing, air-kissing formality to be endured when the guests ranged from obscure European royalty to heads of state and the elite of Europe.

For one day the eyes of the world were focused on Vela Main, though not ones in helicopters. The capital had been designated a no-fly zone for the duration. The security was so extreme that he was surprised the sun got to shine without a permit. This was a day that might have looked to have been miraculously thrown together in two weeks, but in reality it had been planned in the minutest of details for the past five years. The only thing they'd needed was a date for the wedding machine to swing into action. There was a contingency plan for everything, including the possibility that the bride might have put on a hundred pounds or was six months pregnant.

The only point of friction was the presence of the television cameras. Just how much did they want to share with the world's media? How much of an air of mystery did they want to retain? In the end a compromise had been reached—it had been decided the cameras would not be allowed to film the service itself. A small blessing considering they would film everything else.

His head lifted from his contemplation of the floor and his private reflections on the general awfulness of weddings, and this one in particular, when a side door closed behind the last of the florists.

Was it the silence or the atmosphere? He had no idea, but suddenly there was no hiding place for the thoughts that he had been running from. The ones he had refused to acknowledge.

Suddenly the thing he was running from was right there, an inescapable fact, the reason he had moved heaven and earth not to be here today, had actually *invited* his father's wrath. The fact of the matter was that he could barely look at his brother without wanting to knock him down. He was jealous.

Sebastian believed all things to be transitory but that didn't alter the fact that he *wanted* Sabrina. It actually went beyond wanting; it was a *yearning*! Hell, he had less control than he'd had as a hormonal teenager!

Was there some perversity in his DNA that made him want the things he could not have? And then, when forced to recognise it, going out of his way to prove to himself and the world that he didn't want it?

It was a lot less painful than being told you couldn't have something.

His wry smile was tinged with sadness as his father's voice drifted into his head, not just the words but the intonation preserved perfectly in his memory from years ago. He'd just turned fifteen and his brother seventeen…

'Sebastian, you will not go to the briefing next week with your brother.'

He could recall the kick-in-the-gut feeling; he had been hoping for a paternal pat on the back.

'He will ask you and you will say no. Do you understand?'

Sebastian hadn't understood. Luis had begged him to go with him in the first place, after the first weekly briefing he'd attended had, as he'd gloomily told his younger brother, been a nightmare. It had gone on for hours, been so boring that Luis had almost fallen asleep, but he hadn't been able to because the senior palace officials had kept asking him what he thought.

Luis had thought it a massive waste of time.

Sebastian had loyally tagged along, expecting the worst, and it was true that some of the discussions had gone over Sebastian's head, but the complexities discussed had not intimidated him, and he had been a lot less reticent than Luis when asked for an opinion.

His father had come into the room halfway through and sat as a silent observer. Hadn't he seen how well he'd done?

'These meetings are for your brother. They're part of *his* training. One day he will be King, our people will look to him. He needs to stand on his own feet. Do you think he did that today?'

'No, Father. Actually I'd prefer to play cricket anyway. Poor Luis, I expect he'd prefer that as well.' He'd made himself believe it because lying to himself was better than envying his brother.

Well, he hadn't been playing cricket for the last two weeks, but he had thrown himself wholeheartedly into enjoying the pleasures his brother could not. He had made a point of being photographed falling out of exclusive night spots in several time zones.

The media had loved it: headlines spoke of his debauchery; there had been two kiss-and-tell stories that he had been asked to confirm or deny. The truth was, neither of the enterprising ladies in question had made it as far as his bed, and neither had any of the other women snapped falling out of nightclubs and climbing into the back of limos with him.

Sebastian had slept solo, despite the seething sexual frustration that dominated his every waking moment.

The more he tried not to think of Sabrina, the more she dominated his thoughts. Her face, her lips, her body. Under normal circumstances the solution would have been simple, but, as taking her to bed was not an option, instead he focused on her faults, calling her dedication to duty an inclination towards martyrdom, her innocent air artificial, her stubbornness infuriating. But the exercise simply made him more aware of his own faults—the difference being his were real.

She was a person ruled by duty and he was a person ruled by selfishness.

It would have made life a lot easier if he could have seen what Luis appeared to when he looked at Sabrina. The problem was he didn't see what Luis saw—in fact his brother's blindness was another source of frustration. The man had been handed a gift and he acted as if he were some sort of victim. There was a black irony—his brother did not appear to really want her, while he… He shook his head. It really didn't matter what he wanted; the bottom line was he couldn't have it.

'Sir?' So deep in his own thoughts, Sebastian hadn't heard the door open.

He turned his head and saw one of his brother's newer aides standing there. He read nothing into the man's worried frown. For all he knew impending doom might be the man's natural expression.

'Your brother asked that I should deliver this to you by hand.'

Sebastian looked at the handwritten envelope the man was holding out to him.

'Thank you.' A note from Luis? When he would be here soon? He glanced at his watch and realised that his brother should be here now.

Refusing to acknowledge the stirrings of unease in the pit of his stomach, Sebastian slid a finger under the seal and withdrew the single piece of paper.

By the time you read this I will be married. It is better that you don't know where I am.

Sebastian's eyes moved rapidly over the handwritten lines, his emotions shifting from disbelief to shock to fury.

White under his tan, a pulse beating like a sledgehammer in his temple, he got halfway through the rest of the letter before a growl escaped the confines of his throat. He screwed the paper up and tossed it away and stood there, eyes closed, his breath dragging in and out. Only respect for where he was keeping the litany of curses inside his head as he clawed his way back to some sort of control.

His brother had *skipped town*!

Sebastian's gaze went to the altar, where moments before he had imagined his brother kneeling beside a veiled Sabrina.

He felt a stab of guilt. He had wanted it not to happen and now it wasn't, but the cost of his wishes coming true was Sabrina's humiliation.

Sabrina! Did she know? Had his brother sent her a handwritten note too? He was suddenly ready to punch his brother, except Luis was somewhere else, with the love of his life, leaving the rest of them to pick up the pieces.

He bent to pick up the rejected missive, uncreased the paper before he read it again, skimming over the initial sentences.

Better that he didn't know? *Better for you,* thought Sebastian, *because if I did know I would follow you and throttle you, brother!*

He skimmed over the next section, which basically praised and defended the woman his brother had eloped with.

Gretchen is a marvellous woman—you'd love her—but people will tell you things about her. She's had a hard life...the drugs were her escape from abuse. She has never tried to hide anything from me.

Pity, Sebastian thought, directing his silent response to his absent brother, *you cannot say the same!* But of course there had been clues. It no longer seemed incomprehensible that Luis had seemed determined to find fault with Sabrina when clearly she was everything a man could wish for.

His brother, his *dutiful* brother, had been clinging to his forbidden love. Ironic really, he'd been guilty as hell for having feelings he wasn't allowed for his brother's bride while his brother had been pining for another woman. Presumably more than pining.

I didn't want to hurt anyone, but in the end it was simple. I can't live without her. By now Dad will have received my letter of official abdication. He'll need you.

I've told him, Seb, that I'm not his biological son. I hope that will make it easier for him. For both of you.

I know you never understood how I'd begun to forgive him for the way he treated Mother, but I didn't forgive him. I forgave myself for not being able to protect her—you never did.

Abdication. The word jumped out at him from the page as Sebastian felt a totally unexpected stab of sympathy for his parent. His father was going to be devastated. Luis had always been the real son, the one he had put all his hopes for the future in.

Everything I do is an act, it always has been, and I can't do it any more. I would have made a terrible king, it always should have been you, and now it is.

You can stop pretending that you can't do everything better than me. I've been pretending. But so have you, Seb.

Sebastian's chest heaved even after he had read the words. He hardly took in the full implication of his brother's letter, not realising even now that his own life was about to change for ever. Instead what struck him was the omission in the note.

Sebastian turned the page over, unable to believe that his brother had not spared a single sentiment of regret about Sabrina, the woman he had left very publicly standing at the altar.

'Highness.'

Sebastian turned to find one of his father's private secretaries standing in the place that had moments earlier been occupied by his brother's staffer.

'Your father wishes to speak to you.'

Sebastian got to his feet. 'He knows?'

The man tipped his head.

'And how is he?'

'He is most…distressed.'

The last occasion he had been summoned to his father's offices Sebastian had been left to cool his heels in an outer office for half an hour. On this occasion the doors to his father's rooms were open and he was shown straight in.

Sebastian struggled to contain his shock. King Ricard had always worn his sixty years comfortably, and, other than the thickening around his middle and the grey showing in his neatly trimmed beard, he looked much as he had done twenty years ago, but he seemed to have aged visibly since the previous evening.

'Luis—'

'I no longer have a son called Luis, and you have no brother.' The King brought his fist down on the desk, glared at his younger son then turned away but not before Sebastian, who had initially stiffened at the autocratic decree, had seen the sheen of tears in his father's eyes.

Hell, the old man had lost his favourite son and the

legacy he wanted to leave in one fell swoop! He wanted to be remembered by history as the King who had re-unified the island, and he could see that dream slipping away.

'Are you all right?'

His attempt at sympathy was greeted with a pithy retort. 'A bit late in the day to show concern for my well-being. But how I am feeling is not important. The future of our line, my legacy, the reunification is what is important. You and he, you connived...*you* knew he was not my son. I suppose you both thought it was a revenge for your mother. I know you both blamed me... that woman... *I loved her*!'

The last anguished words seemed ripped from him, leaving a shocked silence in their wake.

Sebastian had thought that this day couldn't hold more shocks and now this?

'Yet, you made her miserable.' Luis was right: of all the things their father had done, that was the *one* that Sebastian had never been able to forgive. As for forgiving himself, how could he? Why should he? He had watched his mother die, slowly, by inches and had been helpless to stop what was happening. He *should* have been stronger.

'Do you think *I* was happy? She never loved me. I knew that. I was willing to turn a blind eye to the affair and then it was out and I... None of this is important now. What is important is saving our plans. Reunification is the only thing that matters. We must think ahead—delay would be disastrous.'

'The Summervilles—have they been told?'

'The Duke is furious, and I don't blame him.'

'How is Sabrina?'

His father's heavy brows knitted. 'Who?'

His jaw clenched. 'The bride.'

'Oh, well, upset, I assume. I doubt if she knew about this woman so it must have come as a shock.'

The implication took a few moments to sink in. 'But you did?'

An expression of irritation flicked across the older man's face. 'Do you think I do not always have eyes on you both?' he sneered. 'I *know* you did not actually have an affair with that married woman last year, though you seemed content to allow the world to think the worst of you,' he observed drily.

Sebastian gave an impatient shrug; none of this was news to him. 'This isn't having your spies report back on my love life so you can stay ahead of the game. You knew that Luis was in love with someone else and still you pushed him into marriage.'

The condemnation made no impact on the King. 'I knew he'd had an affair with a woman with an unsavoury past. I asked him to stop. I knew he had slipped,' he admitted. 'He actually wanted to tell the… Sabrina, but we talked him off the ledge.'

'How long has this been going on?'

'Around two years.'

Sebastian sat down in a chair. 'I don't believe this.'

'Unlike you, he was discreet.'

Sebastian's head lifted. 'So it's all right so long as no one finds out? You pushed him into marriage. Did it never strike you as unfair to—?'

His father flashed him a look from under lowered brows. 'He promised me it was over and I believed him.'

Sebastian's anger vanished as his father swayed, the pallor of his face acquiring a grey tinge that sent a slug of fear through Sebastian. 'Are you all right?'

'I'm fine.' The older man sank into a chair, shrugging off his son's helping hand irritably. 'I am not about to hand over my crown any time soon.'

'I don't want your crown.'

The King gave a laugh that ended with a wheeze. 'Are you so sure about that? You were always the one that people looked to. Your brother… No, you have no brother. I have no son…the *bastard* is gone!' He broke off, gasping as his lips turned bluish.

'I'm going to call a doctor.' Before he could raise his voice to call for the help that would undoubtedly be stationed outside the door, his father grabbed Sebastian's arm to get his attention. The fact that his hand was shaking shocked Sebastian in some way more than every other shock the day had delivered.

'No, just get me the bottle out of that drawer.'

Sebastian opened the drawer. 'This?'

His father nodded. 'One under my tongue.' After a moment he nodded. 'That's better.'

'How long have you been ill?'

'I am not ill.'

Sebastian handed him a glass of water. 'How long?'

'It is just angina.'

It seemed to Sebastian that *just* and *angina* were not two words that ought to be used in the same sentence.

'Did Luis know?' He hoped bleakly that the reply would be no, because the brother he loved and admired could not do what he had knowing their father had a heart complaint.

'He needed to know. He was the heir.'

'And I did not?'

'You didn't want to know, but now you have no choice. You, God help us, you are the future of our country.'

Sebastian's gaze lifted upwards but the elaborate

ceiling with its raised relief panels stayed where it was thirty feet above his head. The impression that it was inexorably lowering was an illusion; his cage had no bars, no locks. He would be expected to enter of his own free will. The devil had come to claim him.

'So no pressure, then.'

'Do not be flippant, Sebastian.'

The comment wrenched a hard laugh from Sebastian. 'You expect me to step up, just like that?'

'I expect you will do your duty. Your trouble is everything came too easily to you. Unlike your *brother* you never had to work at anything. That, and your problem with authority.' A laugh rumbled in his chest. 'You *are* the authority now.' The thought seemed to amuse the King for a moment at least before he turned to the matter in hand.

'Count Hugo is briefing the press now. I want you to make an announcement to the guests. It is very important that we are on the same page to minimise the damage, so we will liaise with the Summervilles, smooth things over. Your stepmother is with them now, then, after a decent interval, it can be announced that you and the girl… Sabrina…have decided to get married.'

'I always knew you were ruthless but the human factor, does it actually matter?'

'The *human factor* as you call it is a luxury we do not have. It is one of the things we sacrifice for the privilege of being who we are.'

'Don't you think that after this Sabrina might have other ideas? That she might not like to be moved like a pawn on a board?'

'She is not a pawn, she will be Queen, and if you think her parents are less committed to this than we are, you are wrong.'

Sebastian turned his head from his father to stare at the wall beyond, where light filtered through stained-glass panels of the window left a shifting, shimmering rainbow effect on the stone wall. He took a deep breath and pushed beyond the static buzz of adrenaline overload, fighting to contain the sense of helpless anger he felt surging inside him.

It was ironic—in some ways this was the opportunity he had always imagined, the definitive moment when he could throw his father's expectations and duty back in his face!

Now it was happening and as much as he wanted to reject his father's certainty, as much as he wanted to yell, *'To hell with duty,'* and walk away, he couldn't. He could fight against the duty, but in the end he would do what was expected. The realisation came with a crushing sense of dread…and not just for him.

'Did anyone ask Sabrina what she wants to do?'

'She knows her duty, just as you do, right?' The King did not pause to allow Sebastian space to answer. 'Right now this is about damage limitation. Do you know where your brother is?'

'I thought I had no brother.'

'If he is going to speak to the press I need to know.'

'You mean you need to silence him.'

'I mean to reason with him through an intermediary. I might be willing to continue his generous allowance. Not everyone is as pig-headed as you are, Sebastian.'

CHAPTER SIX

SABRINA STOOD IN a corner.

Her mother stood in the middle of the room in floods of tears and Chloe was providing a shoulder to cry on. Queen Katherine was offering her a glass of brandy, almost as large as the one she was drinking herself.

Her father was standing, his back turned to her, deep in conversation with Luis's private secretary and a group of palace officials. The conversation was not private; her father's comments could probably be heard a mile away.

People seemed to have forgotten she was there.

She really wished she weren't. She closed her eyes and imagined herself in the mountains, the wind in her face, the… A throb of pain in her hand dragged her back to the moment.

Her fingers, which were curled in a death grip around the scrunched-up paper, were white. She lifted her hand to her chest and flexed them to encourage blood back into the cold extremities.

With no pockets in her wedding dress to tuck the letter into, she transferred it to her other hand. She had read it three times before it had made any sense. Actually it still didn't, but she had finally gone to her mother's room and announced that the wedding was off, would someone tell the guests?

'Last-minute nerves, darling. I remember it well. Oh, my, you look beautiful and that shade of lipstick really suits you. The flowers will be—'

'No, Mum, it's really off. Luis has left—there's a letter. He loves someone else apparently and he can't live without her.' She didn't add that Luis had revealed the secret of his parentage, that he and not Sebastian was the bastard.

'Don't be silly, darling.'

'He's abdicated.'

The word seemed to penetrate. It had done the same for Sabrina when it had leapt out from the page; it had made her go back and read it again. The shocking contents evoked a multitude of emotions; humiliation was there and with it relief, a relief that made her feel guilty. She had been given her life back, her freedom, but at what cost?

'But he can't do that. You're going to be the next Queen.' Her voice rose with each successive word until *Queen* emerged as a screech that hurt Sabrina's ears. And not just her ears; belatedly aware of the open-mouthed audience, Sabrina got to her feet, shooing away the team of make-up artists who were putting the finishing touches to the Duchess's face.

Her mother didn't react to their expulsion. 'Dame Olga is singing at the service. She turned down a concert at the Met to be here. Call your father—let him sort things out.'

'I don't think it can be sorted out, Mum.'

'What did you do?'

The unexpected attack made Sabrina back away.

'What did you say to make him do this? Did you say you wanted to carry on working? I knew it! I said to your father that it was a mistake to allow you to have a career… Here he is now.' She gave a sigh of relief as the door opened.

Her father, flanked by senior members of his staff, stood in the doorway. The expression on his florid, good-natured face was grim.

The Duchess's wail was muffled by the hands she pressed to her face.

'Pull yourself together, Olivia,' her husband snapped unsympathetically. 'We need to limit the damage. Where is…? Oh, there you are, Sabrina. At least one person isn't falling apart,' he approved. 'We can't talk here. Come down to the…?' He raised a stern questioning brow at one of the palace staff that had entered with him.

'The King instructed me to make the south salon available, Your Grace.'

So here they all were in the south salon and after half an hour all the talk was going pretty much nowhere.

Sabrina looked at the clock ticking away in a corner, her eyes fixed on the hypnotic swing of the pendulum. She knew she should be feeling more; she was after all the person who had been humiliated. Something she was not likely to forget as her mother kept screeching the information at her every few minutes.

Would anyone even notice if she weren't here?

She unclipped the veil—a family heirloom—and dropped it to the floor. She would have stripped off her finery there and then if she could have but then someone might notice she was there. A naked woman in the room generally got attention.

She fought the temptation to tear at the tiara that felt heavy on her head, and the saucy blue garter, her sister's contribution, had slipped down her thigh. It was all so wrong, even before Luis had followed his heart.

And now, even though she knew it would be considered treasonous by many to even think it, she admired him for having had the guts to walk away. His dumped bride was probably the only person in the room who felt some sympathy for his decision.

But then she knew what it felt like to agree when you wanted to scream no. She knew what it felt like to do your duty. Luis had done what she hadn't had the strength to do. He'd been honest, but how would he live with the guilt?

Suddenly the need to escape the room became overwhelming. If she stayed in it any longer she'd *explode*!

The men stationed outside the door continued to look ahead as she slipped past.

She wanted to go home.

'Sabrina!'

She ignored the voice and began a perilous descent of the spiral steps, going far too fast for someone wearing three-inch heels.

The palace was a maze and built on a massive scale but she was pretty sure that she was headed for the stables. After that her plan was a little hazy but so far plans had not worked out so well for her—maybe it was time to wing it.

'Sabrina, stop!'

She heaved a sigh, grabbed the wooden balustrade and tilted her head back to view her sister, who stood resplendent in the sea-green silk froth of her bridesmaid dress.

'Sabrina, what are you doing?'

'I don't know.' Her expression blank, she looked at the piece of crumpled paper in her hand—actually, she felt blank inside. She cleared her throat. 'It was getting a bit…hot in there for me. I need some fresh air.'

'Outside is probably not the best place to be. There are several hundred guests being—'

'Told the groom has bolted before the stable door closed and, speaking of stables, I think this staircase leads to the stables. There aren't going to be any guests there.'

'It does, but you should come back. They are—'

Sabrina shook her head, cutting her sister off. 'Whatever *they* want me to do the answer is no. Just for today I want a day off from doing and saying the responsible thing.'

Chloe, her skirt hitched high, skipped lightly down the stairs to join her. 'Fair enough. Well, I'd be delighted to tell them to go and stuff it, or I could run away with you. Are you up for this?'

'Why not?'

Her sister's eyes widened. 'I never expected you to say yes,' she admitted.

'So you didn't mean it?'

Chloe laid a hand on her arm. 'Oh, I meant it!' She took the next step herself and paused. 'Mum is sorry, you know, that she yelled. She just panicked.'

'Like Luis—actually, not like Luis. I don't think he panicked. I think he came to his senses. He loves someone else.'

'Fair enough, and, for the record, in your place I wouldn't be so understanding. If he was going to come to his senses why didn't he do it last week or last year or even yesterday? Why leave it until now? It's—'

'A total nightmare,' Sabrina agreed, thinking guiltily of the light at the end of the tunnel.

'Did you guess that he was going to?'

Sabrina shook her head. 'I didn't have a clue.' She expelled a sigh. 'I just need some breathing space.'

'I can do better than that.' Chloe made a grand-reveal gesture as they walked around the corner. 'I always have an escape route. I had a date with a couple of friends last night…after Mum's curfew. We parked here. You fancy a drive?'

'They are not cars,' Sabrina said, looking at the two shiny monsters sitting there. It didn't even occur to her to ask where the owners were as she stared at the dazzling chrome.

'Didn't I tell you I've been learning?' Chloe picked a helmet off the first motorcycle and began to clip it on. 'It's actually quite easy.'

'You want me to sit on the back of that wearing this?' She gestured down at the acres of fitted white silk moulded to her body.

Chloe, hitching up her green skirt, was already clambering onto the first machine. She tossed her sister a set of keys and nodded to the second helmet. 'No, I expect you to follow me on that one,' she retorted, revving the engine of the bike she had climbed onto.

'That's mad, Chloe.'

'True, but if you're not going to be mad today when are you going to be mad, Brina? Come on!'

Sabrina stood there, shaking her head. 'I couldn't.' Her eyes lifted to her sister. *'Could I?'*

'Last night we went for a swim at a little beach just along from the Roman ruins where you opened that yawn-a-minute exhibition on Saturday.'

'Swimming?'

She knew there had to be several dozen legitimate reasons that this was a bad idea but at that moment her brain could only come up with one. 'I don't have a swimsuit.'

Chloe grinned. 'We didn't have swimsuits last night. It is a very private beach.'

* * *

His father had made it as far as the door when his breathing got a lot worse. The doctor, called against his father's wishes, said that bed rest was called for as a *precaution*.

It was half an hour later when Sebastian, deputising for the King, a first, was leaving the room when he encountered someone he vaguely recognised as the Duke's aide, a man who bowed excessively and smiled a lot.

'Highness.' The man sounded breathless, his bow perfunctory and big politician's smile absent. 'Are they here?'

'Are who here?'

'Lady Sabrina and Lady Chloe? We have no idea where they have gone and the Duchess is quite distressed. She has decided they have been kidnapped.'

'Considering the level of security here I seriously doubt it. I have an idea, though. Leave it to me,' he said, leaving the gasping man standing there staring after him as he strode off purposefully down the corridor, punching in the number of the head of security as he walked.

It was picked up immediately.

'The *delicate* security breach we discussed last night?'

'Lady Chloe and the other bridesmaids reached their rooms safely, sir. They remained unaware of the security presence.'

'And you left the motorbikes where they were?'

'We did. Is there a problem?'

One problem? Now that really would be a luxury, Sebastian thought as he took the staircase on his left. It led directly to the stables, where last night Chloe and her friends had naively imagined they had foiled the palace security.

The oil spots on the floor showed where the motor-bikes had stood and the wheel treads in the dusty straw the direction they had gone.

Jaw clenched in frustration, he closed his eyes, but before the curse could leave his lips a muffled sound brought his eyes open. Head tilted to one side, he waited and was rewarded by another noise. It took him a few seconds to track the sound to its source.

He found a piece of torn silk before the rest of the dress and the person wearing it. His initial flare of gut-tightening alarm faded as he realised that Sabrina, who stood beside a motorbike that was lying on its side, having first collided with a wall, was not injured. The same could not be said of the motorbike.

'I hope you're insured?'

Sabrina jumped as though she'd been shot and spun round, brushing the sections of her hair that had escaped the carefully constructed top knot from her eyes as she adopted a defensive attitude. 'It's not mine,' she said, fighting the weirdest compulsion to walk straight into his arms. Skinny dipping was one thing, giving into that impulse would have been taking recklessness to another level.

Still, she'd thought about it, which was bad enough.

I am clearly in a worse condition than I thought, she realised, because any woman who thought safety and comfort lay within those strong arms needed therapy and lots of it!

'Chloe said it was easy.' She sniffed, casting a look of loathing at the motorbike. 'It isn't. I can't do anything right, not even run away…' Her voice quivered with self-pity as she felt an angry splash of tear on her cheek. She swiped it away with a hand and glared at him.

His lips twisted into an ironic half-smile. 'You just

thought you'd slip quietly away on the back of a motor-bike wearing *that*?'

Following the direction of his gaze, Sabrina looked down and felt a stab of guilt when she thought of the skilled women who had sewn the thousands of seed pearls onto the acres of white silk. The beautiful dress was trashed! There were several smears of dirt, oil or both on the bodice and a massive rip in the skirt from when she had tried and failed to mount the motorbike before it had taken off without her.

'Chloe managed it.' Her dismay spiked again when she thought of her sister. 'She's going to be wondering where I am. She'll be worried. She'll think I've done something stupid.'

'As opposed to riding on a motorbike in your wed-ding dress? Don't worry, I'll send someone to tell her you're all right.'

Sabrina shook her head, her lips firming into a mu-tinous line. 'I don't want to *send* someone. I want to go with her. I know they've sent you to take me back.' She folded her arms across her heaving chest and looked up at him, defiance shining in her brown eyes. 'But I won't go.'

He studied her, reading the determination in her tear-stained face, and felt a strong beat of sympathy.

'Did you know?' she asked suddenly. 'That he was going to do it?'

'No, I got a note.'

She nodded. 'So did I.' She held out the crumpled piece of paper. 'Did you know there was someone else?'

His jaw tightened. 'No.'

'Ah, well,' she sighed. 'It's over now.'

Maybe it was a blessing that she actually believed that; he doubted she could cope with the truth. The question was, could he? 'Come on,' he heard himself say.

She blinked. 'Where?'

'Where did you plan to run away to with Chloe?'

'The beach…the one past the Roman dig. We were going swimming.'

'OK.'

She blinked. 'What do you mean?'

'I mean,' he said, 'that I will take you to join Chloe.' He spread his hands wide as she continued to look at him with suspicion. 'No catch.' Without waiting to see if she followed him, he headed for the row of garages where his brother kept his cars. The doors were open and he approached the first one.

He pulled the dust cover off a sporty two-seater. 'It's Luis's,' he said without turning. He had heard the sound of her heels on the cobbles behind him. 'He never locks it.' Sebastian had no compunction about taking it. Luis had gifted him his life and his bride, not that she realised it yet, so he supposed the car was his too.

As she followed Sebastian the irresponsibility of this course of action was beginning to hit home. Running away achieved nothing.

He turned and arched a brow. 'You coming?'

She rocked back a little on her spiky heels as they sank into the gravel. 'I should really go back.'

He didn't proffer an opinion, just stood there looking at her. She took a deep breath and made a choice of the middle ground. 'All right, we'll go and find Chloe and then come back.'

The engine purred into life while she was still manoeuvring herself into the low seat and she released a small squeal as it sped off as she closed the door.

Avoiding the chaos that it seemed safe to assume

surrounded the main entrances to the palace, Sebastian drove through the unguarded stable entrance, past the neatly fenced paddocks, empty today while the staff were attending the celebrations.

Sabrina stayed silent until they reached the hairpin bends that surrounded this part of the island's coast. 'Luis said something in his letter.'

His blue eyes flickered briefly her way.

'Is it true? The King isn't his father?'

'Does it matter now?' He dismissed the question with a curt flick of his head. 'And Luis was an idiot for telling you and…telling anyone,' he condemned.

She was bemused by his attitude. She had seen with her own eyes how his father behaved towards him and she could imagine what effect the headlines about his mother's affair and the rumours of his birth had had on the life of a boy at public school.

'But people said things about you, wrote things. You could have told them the truth.'

'I have a thick skin and I totally believe the old adage what doesn't kill you makes you stronger. It doesn't bother me what people say, or think. They will always find something to write. It would have been harder for Luis.'

She shook her head and wondered if he had told himself that so many times he actually believed it.

'What's happening?' she asked, sliding down in her seat, feeling conspicuous in her white wedding dress as the car slowed to a crawl. Before Sebastian responded to the question they came to a complete standstill.

'I'm not sure,' Sebastian admitted, tapping his fingers on the steering wheel before he opened the window and leaned out. That was when he smelt the smoke… acrid and unmistakable.

'Wait there.'

She craned her neck as Sebastian, with long-legged ease, exited the car and approached one of the several people who had already left their cars. Some were pointing, and then she saw the plumes of smoke rising from behind the hill ahead. Sabrina's stomach muscles quivered as she clambered out and, skirt in hand, ran towards Sebastian, oblivious to the stares her outfit was attracting.

Sebastian stopped, suggesting to drivers they pull their cars as far to the side of the road as possible to give access to rescue vehicles, and turned to her. 'I said to wait inside the car.'

She ignored the statement. 'What's happening? Do you think Chloe...?'

He laid both hands on her shoulders; the heavy contact was somehow comforting. 'There is nothing to be gained from jumping to conclusions. I'm just going to go find out what's happening. You wait here. I'll be back as soon as I can.'

Several other drivers were already jogging down the road but Sebastian hit the ground running, passing them all in moments.

It didn't cross her mind to obey his instructions, but by the time she had rounded the bend ahead and the scene of devastation several hundred yards on was revealed there was no sign of him among the wreckage.

Was Chloe in that?

Battered by fear, her heart thudding, the sound of distant sirens in her ears, Sabrina ran on past a large tanker that was slewed across the road, totally blocking it both ways. She stopped and looked around. It was like some sort of war scene you saw on the TV. Some of the people from the concertina of cars either side of the tanker that were lining the road were standing in the road looking dazed and some were stretched out on the floor. Underfoot was the crunch of broken glass, everything grey in the pall of smoke that made her throat ache and eyes sting.

One distant car was already on fire, sending plumes of orange into the air, increasing the stench of smoke and fuel. If the fire reached the tanker... She pushed away the tendrils of panic and tried to think as, icy cold inside, she ran on past the groaning, blood-spattered victims.

The air left her lungs in one long hissing sigh of relief when she spotted Sebastian; even at fifty feet his tall, commanding figure was easy to spot. It was a couple of seconds later before she saw that he was carrying a figure. She had barely registered the green dress when there was a loud explosion, strong enough to knock one of the men standing close to Sebastian off his feet.

Sebastian swayed but managed to keep on his feet, not really registering the pain of the metal shard that sliced through his cheek. It wasn't until he pushed himself forward that he saw the spark. Before he could brush it away it ignited Chloe's dress.

He dropped her down on the ground and tore off his jacket, smothering the flames before they took hold. Another man joined him until the fire was extinguished.

Chloe opened her eyes and looked up. 'Wow, you look awful...is that smell me? Mum is going to be furious about the dress.'

'It's OK. You're OK,' he said, hoping that it was the truth but in reality he didn't have a clue.

'Sebastian!'

The sound was almost drowned out by the whirr of helicopter blades above their heads.

Sebastian turned his head towards the cry and saw her running, stumbling, dodging the obstacles in her path. Sabrina was yelling something but he couldn't make out the words above the helicopter and roar in his ears.

He got to his feet and swayed; he could make out Sabrina's face now. See her mouth move, but the words and sounds of sobs and everything else were drowned out by the shrill whine of sirens as a fleet of ambulances and fire engines arrived on the scene en masse.

That was the last thing he heard before the ground came up quite quickly to meet him.

CHAPTER SEVEN

LATER THE SEQUENCE remained blurred in her mind. She remembered seeing Sebastian, then the blood that covered half his face, and she watched him fall, and then in her head it happened again and again until finally she got his name out.

'Sebastian!' Her cry sounded that way in her head but came out as a croak as she began to stumble past the debris that littered the area, her progress frustratingly slow across to where he lay—where he lay very still.

Heart drumming, dread like an icy hand around her heart, she knelt down to where he was lying face down, his head turned away from her. One arm was curved above his head, the other trapped under him.

He groaned and she felt a rush of relief that made her sob. 'You're alive. Oh, God, don't die, don't die…please, Sebastian! Help, someone, please, he's…'

A wave of horror rolled over her; the extent of the destruction was too much for her to take in…too much… It was like the set of a disaster movie's big scene only it wasn't a movie—it was *real*.

On her knees she moved towards where her sister lay a few feet away, her eyes closed. Nobody had heard her cry for help, they were busy crying, wailing, bleeding or dying, but she tried again.

'Help!'

Her throat was raw by the time someone heeded her cry.

A man with a torn shirt, his face smoke-blackened, appeared.

He dropped down beside Sabrina and felt her pulse. She shook away his hand—couldn't he see she was fine?

'You're going to be OK.'

'My sister... Sebastian...' She touched her sister's hair and nodded to where Sebastian lay close by.

She watched, her fingers on Chloe's comfortingly strong pulse, as the Good Samaritan began to turn Sebastian over. He was halfway through the procedure before she realised what even someone with a scrap of first aid knew—and she was a doctor.

She was a doctor!

She left Chloe and grabbed the man's arm. 'No, don't! He might have a spinal injury. He needs to be—'

The man stopped, not in response to Sabrina's urgent plea but at the terrible groan that issued from Sebastian.

The sound cut through Sabrina like glass. 'You're hurting him!' she wailed.

His hand fell away. 'Sorry. I was only trying to help.'

They both turned as Sebastian completed the manoeuvre himself before sliding back into unconsciousness.

The man beside her swore as he stared at Sebastian's face. 'That's a mess.'

Sabrina clenched her fists and hissed a fiercely protective denial. 'He's fine...oh, your poor face.' She lifted a shaking hand and, on her knees in the dirt, touched the side of his face that wasn't shredded and bleeding and stroked the dark hair back from his brow.

The man moved away.

'Hey, he's the guy who got the girl from the cliff.'

Two men walking past supporting a staggering woman between them stopped and looked down at Sabrina and Sebastian.

'Hold on, they'll be with you soon…'

'I'm fine, but they—' She stopped, her voice cracking with fear.

The man nearest nodded and raised his voice and yelled, 'One over here, one for triage, severe facial lacs, blood loss, head injury!'

'Brina!'

'Chloe.' Before Sabrina could react to her sister's hoarse whisper two jumpsuit-clad figures reached them. She shuffled out of the way, watching as they examined her sister, inserted a venous line before lifting her onto a stretcher.

When Chloe saw Sabrina she struggled to pull the oxygen mask off her face.

Sabrina covered her sister's hand with her own. 'No, leave it.' Chloe's eyes closed. 'She's my sister,' she explained to the two paramedics as she ran along beside them.

'We'll look after her,' one said. 'She's being airlifted.'

She walked back to where Sebastian lay and stood there watching as her sister was stretchered away to the waiting helicopter. The explosion was deafening.

Sabrina reacted on instinct, throwing herself over Sebastian. She had no idea how long she lay there; her ears were still ringing when two paramedics pulled her off.

One began to examine Sebastian, the other shone a torch in Sabrina's eyes. She pushed his hand away. 'Can you walk?' She nodded.

'Great.' He draped a foil blanket over her shoulders and shouted out, 'A walking wounded over here, guys.'

She lifted her chin. 'No, I'm not leaving him.' She'd let them take Chloe away but enough, she decided, was enough. 'I'm staying with him.'

The tired-looking paramedic sounded irritated by her attitude. 'Look, there are people here who actually do need my help and—'

The young woman crouched beside Sebastian, adjusting the line she had just put in his arm, looked up. 'Have a heart, man, can't you see that they just got married?' She indicated Sabrina's torn and dirty wedding dress.

'This is your wedding day?'

'It was meant to be,' she answered truthfully, thinking that it seemed like a lifetime ago since she had put on her wedding dress.

He swore in sympathy and looked down at his colleague, who was still kneeling beside Sebastian. 'That one ready to move?'

She nodded. 'He's stable, and sats are up to ninety-five…tough guy.'

The man with Sabrina took her arm. 'You can go with him.'

'Thank you,' Sabrina said. Her gratitude even greater when, on the way to the hospital in the back of the ambulance, Sebastian regained consciousness twice and each time it was the sound of her voice that stopped him fighting to free himself from the safety restraints before they had a chance to administer sedation.

Sabrina had not expected their anonymity to last. Admittedly her face, even without the walking-wounded look, was less well known but it seemed inevitable that someone would at some point make the connection between the anonymous injured figure who lay, his famous features swathed in bandages, on the stretcher and their Prince.

But so far no one had and, as it was hard to imagine that their treatment could have been better if the hospital staff had realised they were treating their Prince, it hadn't seemed a priority to explain or correct the myth that they were a newly married couple, which had obviously followed them to the casualty department. While she waited to be seen herself, she was kept up to date with Sebastian's progress. Sabrina knew she would not have been told the results of his CT or any of the other tests if they had known the truth.

As someone who was not his wife or family she would have been told nothing, so she silenced the twangs of conscience, and took comfort from the technicality that she hadn't lied—yet. Unless staying silent could be counted as lying. Should she reveal that under the dirt, blood and injuries the man they were treating was their Prince?

People were kind even rushed off their feet. The staff she asked took time to try and find details about Chloe for her, though on each occasion they had not been able to locate her sister in the system, but then the system had to be at breaking point.

The island boasted some pretty impressive medical facilities, but a major disaster had stretched their resources to the limit.

It remained frustrating that nobody seemed to be able to tell her where her sister was, but her own injuries were minor. She hadn't even known she had any, but the blood seeping from the head wound had caught the attention of a passing nurse. It needed stitching and they insisted on keeping her in overnight.

'I hope you don't mind sharing,' the nurse said as she manoeuvred Sabrina's bed into place beside the occupied one in the room obviously only ever intended to hold one bed.

'Of course not.'

The nurse smiled. 'Not really the way you intended to spend your honeymoon, but we thought…'

Sabrina's eyes flew to the person lying in the bed next to hers.

It was Sebastian, looking much better than when she had last seen him despite the livid bruises visible around the dressing that covered the wound on his face. His hands above the sheet were swathed in bandages too.

'Is he in pain?' she whispered, knowing full well they would have pumped him up with painkillers but needing the reassurance of hearing someone say it.

'No, he's dosed up to the eyeballs so he might be a bit groggy when he wakes up,' the nurse warned. 'The drip is just giving him fluids,' she went on to explain.

Sabrina nodded, glancing at the label on the bag.

The nurse gave her hand an encouraging squeeze. 'He was lucky really. The surgeon who repaired your husband's face is one of the best plastic surgeons there is—not that we don't have good doctors here, but Mr Clare is *the* man. And he was only on the island for the royal wedding, apparently. I wonder how that went. Anyhow, he just turned up here and offered to help out after he heard about what had happened.

'I just thought you should know that your husband had the very best care. I'm sure a doctor will be along to fill you in later but, as you can imagine, we are a bit stretched.'

'Thank you. His hands…?'

'Superficial.'

Her lowering of tension was fleeting as she asked a moment later, 'My sister, Chloe, did anyone…?'

Sabrina read bad news in the girl's hesitation so she was prepared as much as she could be for bad news when it came.

'That would be *Lady* Chloe Summerville?'

Sabrina nodded.

The girl's eyes widened. 'So you're…?'

'I'd kind of prefer to stay below the radar for now.'

The nurse responded to the appeal with a nod and a smile. 'They airlifted your sister to a specialist burns unit on the mainland. I believe your parents went with her…' The girl laid a buzzer on the bed beside her. 'You just ring if you want anything, La— Sabrina.'

Sabrina looked at the buzzer. What she really wanted was to go back to that moment on the staircase when she could have gone, no, *should* have gone back. But that wasn't going to happen because the world was not fair. If it were *she* would be the one living with the consequences of her actions, not Chloe, not Sebastian.

If she could have swopped places she would have in a heartbeat.

That's easy to say, Brina, mocked the voice in her head, *when you know you can't.*

Nurses came in and out during the night to record Sebastian's observations and when they saw she was awake all they told her was that he was *doing fine*.

She lay there counting down the hours on the clock on the wall opposite. It was two in the morning when a dapper man she recognised as the King's private secretary appeared.

He didn't seem to notice Sabrina at first, he was so transfixed by the sight of Sebastian.

He shook his head and gasped, 'Lady Sabrina! You

here, this is…well, it is simply intolerable to expect either you or His Highness to share a room with *anyone* at all.'

'It's fine,' Sabrina said. 'They are pushed for space and I'm going home in the morning. But if there is any news of my sister could you let me know?'

'Of course, so sad, and when we were still reeling from this morning's events. The King is… Well, he wanted to come, but he had an…an event when he heard.'

'Event?'

'A heart event. Not an attack, you understand, but the Queen is at his side and he is comfortable,' he added as if he were reading out a press release—actually he had probably already done so. 'They wanted to be here, but it is lucky they are not here to see their son being treated like an ordinary— Of course, if he had not gone out without his security presence… But, no matter, I will set wheels in motion.'

'At least there are no press hiding behind bedpans to take a snap.'

The man rubbed his chin as he took on board her comments. 'That is certainly a benefit of anonymity, and the idea of the Prince being treated like any of his subjects would be good for his image, presenting him as a man of the people. Well, perhaps for tonight at least we might leave things as they are.' He tipped his head towards the bed where Sebastian slept on. 'Do you know if there will be any scars?'

'I should think so,' she said evenly and closed her eyes. If she had to hear the man thinking out loud of how to put a positive spin on Sebastian being marked for life she would have to throw something at him.

She was so tired of people who thought that the truth

was a dirty word, people who thought through every syllable they uttered, always choosing appearances above honesty.

Sometimes the truth was just the truth, no matter how much you manipulated it, and the truth was that two people she cared for deeply were in pain because of her!

Her eyelids flickered as a series of images ran through her head. Sebastian mocking her, Sebastian aloof, Sebastian kissing her, Sebastian smiling and on and on, always Sebastian.

Was she in any position to condemn anyone for being economical with the truth?

Truth?

Didn't you have to ask the right question first to hear the answer, the truth?

When she opened her eyes the King's private secretary had gone. She looked at the man in the bed beside her own and saw that Sebastian was awake and looking at her, his blue eyes clouded by the drugs in his system. The ache of empathy was so strong that she forgot all about truths and answers.

'Hello,' she said softly.

'I…' He paused and moistened his lips. 'I was looking for Chloe,' he slurred.

She felt tears spring to her eyes. 'You found her.'

'Where is this…?'

'Hospital. You were hurt but you're going to be all right. The room, it's funny…' she said, ignoring the odd aching feeling inside her when she laughed, 'but they think we're married.'

'We are married? Yes, I remember now. I was dreaming about it. I kissed you.' He smiled. 'I remember now you looked beautiful.' Still smiling, he closed his eyes and his breathing showed he was asleep.

Satisfied that he was resting comfortably, she had just drifted off to sleep herself when she was woken.

The man wheeling the chair told her that he had come to take her to CT before discharge.

She glanced towards Sebastian, who was still sound asleep.

'I don't need one.'

'I'm not a doctor, are you?'

She could have said yes but she didn't. 'I could walk.'

'You could, but if you fall over I'm the one who'll get the boot…so…?'

She got in, holding the open back of her gown in place to cover her modesty and her behind.

'I've seen worse,' wisecracked her driver. 'You two the honeymooners? Don't worry, it won't take long and he'll still be here when you get back.'

He was, but not in bed when she walked into the room past the security guards who had been there when she'd left. Her brief flurry of irrational panic subsided when she saw the figure standing in a narrow open door that was a tight squeeze for a broad-shouldered man plus a portable drip stand.

In her absence the big bulky dressing had been removed. In its place was a narrow, almost transparent strip that showed the full extent of his repaired wound. Sabrina was relieved by what she saw. The man who had operated had clearly been as good as the nurse had claimed. Her professional eye could see beyond the bruising and swelling that made his face unrecognisable, and she knew that the healing process would fade the livid raised red scar to silver.

The professional in her saw a good job; the woman in her saw not ugliness, but pain and she winced, her empathy shifting uneasily to dismay. What she was feeling went beyond normal empathy. It wasn't even guilt that she felt; it was more…it was… The name for what she was feeling remained there, just out of reach.

As their eyes met Sebastian's were dark with pain and exhaustion. She ironed her expression out into a smile as her eyes moved in a covetous sweep up the long, lean length of his body. Unlike her he was not wearing hospital issue, although someone kind in the CT department had given her a big towelling dressing gown to cover the open-backed theatre gown. Sebastian, by contrast, was wearing a pair of dark sweats and a T-shirt that revealed the incredible lean muscles of his torso and his powerful biceps. Fighting the hormonal rush, she lowered her eyes.

'Should you be out of bed?'

Sebastian took hold of the drip stand awkwardly in one lightly bandaged hand and began to walk towards her, feeling her eyes on him and knowing what she saw when she looked at him. It had been there in her face in that unguarded moment—he had become a man with a ruined face, someone to pity, someone she would soon learn it was her *duty* to be with, to lie in bed with even if inside she felt disgust.

And Sabrina would never turn her back on her duty.

He turned away as he felt the fury and outraged pride rise in him.

'Well, as you see, I am. The surgeon is apparently due to arrive in…' He glanced towards his wrist and swore, then swore again as he banged the drip stand into the table positioned at the bottom of the bed.

'What's wrong?'

'Nothing is wrong. I've left my watch in the bathroom and this thing is—'

'I'll get it.' Sabrina moved past him into what was little more than a cubicle, clean but utilitarian with a basin, lavatory and shower.

'How are you feeling, really?' she called out as she lifted the metal-banded watch from where he'd left it on the edge of the washbasin.

'Pretty much the way I look. Maybe under the circumstances *pretty* is not the right word.'

The bitterness in his voice made her pause; he could not blame her for what had happened any more than she was blaming herself. If she hadn't run away from her responsibilities her sister and Sebastian would have read about the pile-up in the newspaper.

'The scar will fade, you know.' It sounded like a platitude and one it seemed he had no intention of responding to. Taking a deep breath, she prepared to go back and face his pretty justified anger when the sound of a new voice made her pause.

'Outside, all of you!'

Poised on the point of walking out of the small bathroom, Sabrina instinctively shrank back into the room. The voice was unmistakably that of King Ricard.

'I thought you'd had a heart attack, Father.'

'A slight cardiac *incident*, that's all,' she heard the King correct. 'You look like hell. What were you doing on that road with the Summerville sisters?'

'Going for a swim.'

'Do not t…t…try me, Sebastian.'

'Shall I get that nurse back in here?' No sarcasm this time, but concern roughened the edge of Sebastian's deep voice as his father wiped beads of sweat from his upper lip.

'She's a doctor, not a nurse, and no, it's just overly warm in here.'

'You didn't need to come in person. You could have just sent flowers but I'm touched. I really am.'

'Why is everything a joke with you? This is the sort of attitude that made it necessary for me to come in person. The news that you and the Summerville girls were involved in the pile-up has leaked—inevitable, but annoying. However, there is some good news. They have decided that you were a hero. Don't look at me like that. I don't care if you were not—this is the way people will see you.'

Her back pressed against the white-tiled wall, she could hear the satisfaction in the monarch's voice. An image of her parents sitting beside her sister's bed drifted into her head. The last thing they would be thinking about was how the media spun the story. While in the other room the King had not even asked his son how he was!

'And that is all that matters, the perception not the truth.'

Her eyes widened. It was as if Sebastian had picked up on her own thoughts, though he sounded more warily resigned than angry.

'Do not take that sanctimonious tone with me, Sebastian. You are not some innocent. The royal family is a product and it is our job to promote it. You are my heir.'

'You make it sound so attractive, Father,' she heard Sebastian drawl. 'Has it occurred to you that I might say thanks, but no, thanks?'

'You always thought you could do the job better than me. Now is your chance to prove it.'

'Spoken like a true manipulator.'

'So is there anyone in your life at the moment—a woman?' From her hiding place the King's deep sigh of irritation was audible. 'Fine, it makes no difference, but if there is get rid of her. Later on if you are discreet I see no reason you shouldn't enjoy liaisons, but until you are safely married I want no sniff of scandal. Getting her on side is going to take delicate handling after what your brother did.'

'I thought I did not have a brother.'

The King ignored the interjection. 'The Duke and Duchess,' he continued, 'have become very *sentimental*. Their attitude is most disappointing. I suppose with the other girl in hospital…but hopefully they will rethink in due course. However, as it stands, they say they are not going to force Sabrina to marry you. They say it is *her* choice. So it is your job to make sure she makes the *right* choice. It should not be too hard for you—she has a sense of duty and you have a way with women. Do I make myself clear?'

'Crystal.'

From her hiding place she heard the sneer in Sebastian's voice but his father seemed oblivious to it.

'In some way, you know, this accident could be a blessing. It will keep the wedding story off the front page at least.'

'Spoken like a true narcissist. Pain, suffering and loss—who cares so long as it's useful for us?'

'At least you recognise that there is an *us*… Finally. This royal business we are in, *love* is best kept out of it.'

'You told me you loved my mother.'

'And it never gave me a moment's happiness. What do you want? Oh, for God's sake…'

'Five minutes, I said, Your Majesty.'

'All right, just watch what you are doing with that chair. Sebastian, we will speak later. Do not say anything to the press until you have spoken to Hugo and if anyone calls you a hero try to look modest. Who knows? That scar might even be useful.'

Sebastian waited until the royal party had exited, leaving the original guards outside, and went into the bathroom. Sabrina was sitting on the floor, her knees drawn up to her chin, her back pressed against the tiles as though she had slid down them.

'I am assuming you heard all of that.'

Sabrina lifted her head, pushing her hair back from her face with both hands as she angled a look up at him. There was a remoteness in his face that she found chilling.

'So, I'm going to be passed on to the next brother.'

Who doesn't want me any more than the first one did...

She recognised it was irrational, but for some reason this knowledge was far more painful to her than the humiliation she had suffered at Luis's hands.

The belief that she was doing the right thing had enabled her to take a pragmatic approach to the prospect of a loveless marriage to Luis, but when it came to Sebastian being coerced into taking his brother's reject, Sabrina couldn't be objective. Everything inside her just shrivelled up with horror at the prospect of living a lie with Sebastian; she hated the idea of him resenting her and their life together.

How long would it be before he did as his father had suggested and had a discreet affair?

'You heard him.' Their glances connected. 'You could refuse. It sounds as though your parents have had a change of heart. They have realised perhaps that their daughters' lives are more important than political machinations?' He looked at her and saw the sadness in her dark eyes. 'But you won't, will you? The fact is you won't because you have been brainwashed from birth to be *the sacrifice*. You didn't want to marry Luis but you were prepared to, you were prepared to lie in his bed, let him make love to you while you planned next week's dinner menu.'

'I tried not to think that far ahead.'

She didn't realise until she said it that this was true; she had never once imagined herself in bed with Luis. She had never thought about his naked body, or his mouth or how his skin would feel against hers. But since the first moment she'd seen Sebastian she had not stopped thinking about *all* of those things about him, and a lot more!

She was thinking about them now, and the rise in her core temperature made her glad of the cool of the tiles as she pushed herself up the wall into a standing position. The ache low in her pelvis mocked her weakness while his double standards and his contemptuous attitude made her angry enough to ignore the grey tinge to his skin, the lines of pain bracketing his mouth.

'I don't know why you're angry with me. I didn't hear *you* say no to your father! You have to do something you don't want to—oh, well…boo-hoo! Do you think I *enjoy* feeling like some hand-me-down pair of shoes that never quite fitted to begin with? But, what the hell, they look the part if they cripple you…!'

During her outburst he had stared down at her, then after a couple of beats of silence he laughed, the hard sound devoid of humour.

'No, I didn't, did I?' he drawled slowly, the anger in his cobalt-blue eyes replaced now by a glitter of self-derision. 'I'm actually as surprised as you to discover that I'm not about to take advantage of this heaven-sent opportunity to kick my father when he's down.'

As he inhaled through flared nostrils his chest lifted dramatically, drawing her attention to the telltale triangle of sweat on his T-shirt. Her self-righteous tirade still echoing in her ears, she winced as guilt sliced through her. She had made zero allowances at all for the fact he was clearly in considerable pain, even if he was too damn stubborn to admit it.

He released a long, hissing breath as his glance settled on her face; the look in his eyes made her own breath catch.

If her life had depended on it she could not have broken free of that hypnotic azure stare.

'Shoes…mmm…' Inside her hospital-issued slippers Sabrina's toes curled. 'I don't think so—not even the high-heeled spiky, sexy ones, though I *can* see you in them. Actually you make me think of…' his glance sank to her mouth '…*silk*…' the way he curled the word around his tongue made her shiver '…and I think we could fit very well indeed.' His bandaged hand lifted to the bandaged side of his face. 'If, of course, you are able to overlook this in the dark.'

The last comment shook her violently free of the dry-throated, breathless floating sensation that had gripped her during his earlier throaty comments.

She closed her eyes and clenched her fists, hissing through clenched teeth, 'Yes, because I am a shallow, superficial… Be glad you are injured or, so help me, I'd be kicking you.' She pushed past him and back into the hospital room.

She missed the startled look on his face but heard his laughter and sensed him moving back into the room they had shared last night as she went across to the bed she had slept in and grabbed the plastic bag containing the clothes she had been wearing when she'd arrived.

Clutching the bag to her chest, she slowly turned and instantly forgot what she was about to say. 'Get back into bed.'

'That's a very wifely thing to say.'

She fought the urge to help him, keeping her expression carefully neutral at a grunt of pain that escaped his clamped lips as he eased himself onto the bed.

He pulled out a pillow before easing his long lean length down slowly. By the time he had accomplished the task his skin gleamed with a thin layer of perspiration. 'What, you're not going to plump my pillows?'

'When did you last have analgesia?'

'Does it matter?'

'Being in pain,' she retorted tartly, 'when there is pain relief available does not make you manly, it makes you pretty stupid.'

Privately he conceded she probably had a point. 'Not big on the bedside manner, then.'

I could be.

Shocked by the thought that jumped into her head, she veiled her gaze, clearing her throat before she responded.

'Shall I call a nurse for you?'

'As it's been a full thirty seconds since one applied a cool soothing hand to my brow I think we can assume we won't have to wait long until one appears,' he observed, not sounding very grateful for the attention. 'How about you?'

'I'm fine, barely a scratch,' she admitted guiltily.

'And Chloe?'

'I don't know. She's been transferred to a burns unit.' It certainly put her own problems in perspective. 'It's so unfair. I caused this and Chloe and you are both paying for it.'

He arched a brow. 'How exactly is this your fault?'

'I ran away.' She blinked as her eyes filled with the sting of unshed tears burning.

'It was an accident, Sabrina, a freak set of circumstances. Beat yourself up by all means if you want to, but I suspect that Chloe would benefit from a slightly less self-indulgent response.'

She flinched, the initial flare of indignation at his callous attitude vanishing as she recognised he had a point. She scrubbed her eyes with her knuckles and took a deep breath. 'You're right,' she admitted. 'Mum and Dad are with Chloe. It's where I should be.' Her jaw firmed as she wondered how quickly she could get to them.

Disarmed by the admission that he could not imagine any woman finding herself in Sabrina's position, he studied her face. The tear stains, the bruised smudges beneath her eyes, the honey hair lying loose and tangled—and yet she still looked beautiful. His body, bruised, battered and broken even as it was, reacted to that beauty, the lust tempered with tenderness that struck a chord of shock through him.

'Family loyalty?'

Sabrina's eyes lifted at the soft comment. Her slender shoulders rose in a tiny shrug. 'It's what families do.'

'Your family maybe.'

'Have you and your father…?' she began tentatively.

'Always hated one another?'

She met his gaze steadily. 'I wasn't going to say that.'

'No, I'm sure you were going to be more tactful. My father never forgave me for being born even after he discovered I was actually his son and, unlike Luis, I never forgave him for killing my mother. Oh, not literally,' he admitted in response to her wide-eyed reaction. 'He didn't need to. Perhaps he did *love* her, or his version of it, I don't know, but he sealed her fate the day he married her. She was very young and the marriage was—'

Across the space that separated them Sabrina could feel the emotion rolling off him. Years of anger and resentment that had dominated his childhood and shaped his adult life. 'Convenient,' she inserted quietly. 'What was she like?'

A flicker of surprise crossed his face and for a moment he was silent, as if considering the question. 'Didn't Luis ever speak to you about her?'

She shook her head. 'We never talked much at all.'

He stayed silent as he absorbed this information; something in his expression made her wish she had been less open. 'Delicate,' he said eventually. 'And sensitive, shy. I used to *will* her to stand up to him.' His jaw clenched as he admitted with an air of acceptance she sensed had been a long time coming, 'But she couldn't, it wasn't in her. Ironic really—Luis did what we always wanted her to do: he escaped. But she never did. It was like seeing a wild bird trapped in a cage. Painful, heartbreaking, but you know deep down that even if someone opened the door for her she'd be too scared to fly away.'

The poignant image his words drew made her eyes fill, but as much as she felt for the sad, unhappy woman he described Sabrina felt *more* for her sons. She strongly believed that a mother's job was to protect her children but it seemed the roles had been reversed with Sebastian and his brother. She sucked in a deep breath as she silently vowed that no child of hers would ever feel like that.

'Or, she knew it was her duty to stay,' she suggested quietly. 'I know you think it's a dirty word, but isn't that what you're doing by marrying me?'

'Did you just propose to me, Sabrina?'

Her delicate jaw quivered. 'I expect that that will happen when we're not in the same room by someone who is working on the press release now and it's better that way, isn't it? No pretending, given the circumstances.'

There was no trace of the relief she had anticipated in his expression, but then he was most probably in pain. He certainly didn't object when a nurse bustled in and offered to top up his pain relief.

The effects of the analgesia hit Sebastian almost straight away; within seconds his eyelids were closing, and before a second nurse appeared with a holdall that had arrived with fresh clothes for Sabrina he was asleep.

She changed quietly in the bathroom so as not to disturb Sebastian. On her way to the door she paused and looked down at him. Asleep he looked younger, the lines of cynicism ironed out.

Unable to fight the impulse, she reached out and found her fingers halfway to his cheek before she stopped herself. A quiver of sensation radiated out from the pit of her stomach...not her heart. Gratitude was natural. He had saved Chloe. They had gone through a trauma together.

This was a merger, not a marriage.

CHAPTER EIGHT

LOW-KEY, IT HAD been agreed, was appropriate under the circumstances, and the civil ceremony was just that, a handful of people beyond the immediate family. There were photographs, which would be released along with an official statement to be issued later that week.

So she was married. Sabrina could not decide if she was meant to feel different. She glanced to the man, her husband, who sat beside her. There was a remote, untouchable quality about him that even had she wanted to make conversation would have made her think twice. Sabrina didn't want to.

They were physically inches apart but in every other way worlds apart; the journey passed in total silence, not the companionable variety. He was making no effort to change that.

The only time he had spoken was when they'd got in the car and she had told him that she wanted to go to the hospital to see Chloe. He'd nodded and issued a curt instruction to the driver. Then, when they'd arrived at the hospital, he'd pulled out a laptop.

'I'll wait here.'

So Sabrina had gone into the private London hospital her sister had been transferred to, flanked by two security men, to the room where her sister had spent the last few weeks. Chloe had been scheduled to leave before the wedding, but an infection had meant that the skin grafts on her leg that had sustained injury had not taken and the entire painful process had had to begin all over again.

The amount of suffering her sister had endured made her own situation seem insignificant. She took a deep breath before she went in, donning a smile along with a sterile gown. The guilt she felt was her problem. It was not something she was about to burden Chloe with; her sister had enough to contend with but Sabrina knew it was her fault. If she hadn't run away Chloe would not be lying in a hospital bed.

'Hello, you!'

Chloe was lying in bed, her lower body beneath a cradle arrangement that held the sheet off her skin, her face a little thinner than it had been a few months ago and a lot paler, but her smile was just as bright.

'So, how did it go?'

Sabrina pulled up a chair and did her best to soften the truth with humour.

'Oh, you know—your usual shotgun wedding atmosphere. Without the pregnancy, of course. Lots of glaring and suspicion and a man…actually, four…guarding the door to stop anyone from legging it.'

'Sounds a laugh a minute.'

'It was pretty much what I'd expected and this time the groom turned up, which most people seemed to think a plus,' Sabrina added drily.

'Well, I think you had a lucky escape. Imagine living your life with a man who was in love with someone else.'

The way Chloe was talking it was almost as if she believed that Sebastian loved her. If it made her happy Sabrina saw no reason to correct her.

'So where is the man himself? I forgot to thank him for the fruit basket he brought this morning, so send my love.'

'You saw Sebastian this morning?'

'Didn't he say?'

Say? She swallowed a bubble of hysteria in her throat. 'He must have forgotten.' She was not about to tell her sister that they barely communicated at all.

Had it really been two months since that strange twenty four hours when they had shared a hospital room the night after the accident? She had barely been alone with Sebastian since.

'He comes most mornings—has all the nurses drooling. You do know that if you hadn't married him I would have had him myself, don't you? If he hadn't got me off that cliff I couldn't have held on any longer.' She shuddered. 'I know that nowadays it would be sympathy sex, but—'

'Chloe, don't say that!' Sabrina said, her voice husky with tears. 'The doctors say that the scars will be—'

'They will be scars, and, unlike your husband's, they will not be sexy ones. And while we all know that it's what you're like inside that counts, back in the real world, well…' She gave a sudden deep sigh and wiped her hands across her eyes. She smiled. 'Ignore me, Brina. I'm just having a self-pity day, but Sebastian is a good man, you know, and we have kind of bonded over our scars.'

Sabrina stayed for half an hour before reluctantly leaving her sister.

The sight of the streaks left by dried tears on Sabrina's cheeks when she returned to the car elicited an involuntary stab of protective warmth in Sebastian's chest.

'How is Chloe?' he asked.

'Being brave, but I think she's in pain, though she says not. She thanked you for the fruit.'

He gave a grunt of assent and nodded.

'I'm grateful, Sebastian.'

He stiffened. 'I do not want your gratitude.'

She could almost feel the dignity and calm that she had fought hard to retain all day slipping like sand through her fingers. Except her fingers were clenched so tightly into fists that nothing could have escaped them.

'You don't want a wife,' she blurted, hearing the heavy thud of her pulse like a hammer in her temples as her suppressed anger surged hotly.

Even as she acknowledged it she realised that she had no legitimate right to feel this way. It was no more rational to feel angry now than it had been to imagine that they had made some sort of *connection* that night when they had shared a hospital room.

What had happened since had shown pretty clearly that the only time they were ever going to be *connected* was when he was heavily medicated. She smothered a hysterical bubble of laughter and coaxed some calm into her manner.

'But you've got one. Me, actually, and it's kind of obligatory to talk to her.'

He closed the laptop, the tension of the day and the days that had preceded it stretching the skin tight across his perfect bone structure, a perfection that was emphasised not marred by the scar, already fading to silver, along the right side of his face.

He read the unhappiness and anger in her face and felt a fresh surge of the guilt that had been his ever-present companion over the last weeks. Weeks when he had been the recipient of an immersion programme in all that being the heir apparent involved, and, in the process, feeling a new respect for his brother.

At least he now knew what he was letting himself in for. Sabrina? She was totally unprepared for what was coming, just as his mother had been, and yet had he warned her? Had he opened the door of the golden cage that had now closed? He felt a fresh surge of loathing; he was no better than his father.

'What do you want me to say?' He could have said he wanted her, that he had wanted her from the outset more than he had ever wanted another woman, but wanting did not excuse the fact he had taken advantage of her ignorance. Because he didn't want to do this alone. He felt a flash of guilt.

Pride brought her chin up, but the coldness in his voice hurt more than she was prepared to admit. It was becoming pretty obvious that he didn't require anything from her.

'I think you've said enough.'

Sabrina glanced his way occasionally during the rest of the journey; his stillness was as impregnable as his profile, the shadows as they travelled through the darkness adding emphasis to the strong, sculpted planes as he stared out of the window.

What was he thinking?

It was impossible to tell. Nothing seeped through his mask, only the occasional Arctic-wolf flicker in his arresting blue eyes reminding her of the man he had been two months before. Two months being the time that had finally been considered a *decent* interval between being dumped by one brother and getting married to the next.

She found herself wondering what had happened to, and amazingly feeling a stab of nostalgia for, the *Playboy Prince* who was guaranteed to be in the *right* place saying the *wrong* thing for the cameras, smiling as he put two fingers up to the world in general and the press in particular.

Had that man, the one whose life choices kept the damage-control experts in work, gone for ever? She recalled the soft words he had murmured for her ears only when he had observed her hand shaking while they waited for the registrar's arrival.

'Relax, just treat this day like any other, no different than yesterday, no different than tomorrow. Don't have any expectations—I don't. I expect nothing of you.'

He might not but others did. The King's senior advisor, who had taken her to one side just before the actual ceremony, had reminded her that the fate of a nation was pretty much on her shoulders.

'Prince Sebastian is an unknown factor. He is making an effort but we all know that he is volatile, his history... I know we can trust you, Lady Sabrina, to be a steadying influence.'

'I think it might be better if you trusted the Prince. I will not mention your comments on this occasion, but in future...' She had taken some pleasure from the aide's embarrassed retreat and hoped the message had reached the King that if he wanted to undermine his son she would not be party to it.

The words of an article she had read the previous week profiling the men with power in Europe came back to her. The new Crown Prince was *complex*, the smitten writer had claimed, referring to the glimpses of the barbaric pagan behind the urbane exterior.

Pagan? Not helping, Sabrina, she told herself, pushing away the words. The car suddenly turned off the minor road they had been travelling on for several miles and through big gates that swung open at their approach. The uneasiness in her stomach gave an extra-hard kick as the gates closed behind the car that had travelled at a discreet distance behind them since they'd left London.

The driveway, illuminated at ground level by rows of lights, seemed to go on for miles. Sabrina didn't mind; she was in no hurry to arrive!

Finally they stopped, the uniformed driver pulling up in front of a building with a Georgian façade. This was a private house, not a hotel. Someone had told her who the house belonged to—not that the owners would be here for the duration of their stay. They had been guests at the small ceremony today. Sabrina had been introduced but she couldn't remember their faces or names; it was all part of the blur.

For a full thirty seconds nobody moved except the man who was sitting beside the driver, who spoke into a device attached to his wrist, then he nodded and it seemed as though dark suited and booted figures appeared from everywhere.

Sebastian was already being greeted at the porticoed entrance when someone eventually came and opened the car door for her. By that point, aside from the alert-looking suited figures either side of the entrance, the security presence had vanished.

As she made her own exit she imagined them hidden in the bushes. It wasn't a particularly comforting thought. As she approached the house the feeling that had been with her all day persisted. A weird sense of out-of-body disconnection, as though this were happening to someone else and she were watching. And now she was listening to someone else's heels crunching on the gravel, someone else was feeling the evening breeze carrying the tang of the sea on her face.

But it hadn't been someone else that had said *I do* today. That had been her.

Inside the hall of the house, a magnificent marble-floored space dominated by a great sweeping staircase and lit by several chandeliers, stood *her husband*, his back turned to her. He was deep in conversation with three other men and a woman who was taller than two of the men, and striking with close-cropped white blonde hair set off dramatically against the black trouser suit she wore.

Sabrina could not hear what they were saying but it didn't seem to make Sebastian happy, though he heard them out before he fired off a staccato stream of sentences.

Weirdly she almost envied them—at least he was communicating with them in entire sentences, not gruff monosyllables.

Fighting was better than indifference; she was beginning to wonder if she had ever imagined that he had been attracted to her. It made the fact that just looking at him made her tremble all the more hard to come to terms with—to live with on a daily basis.

Maybe that was what it was. She represented the duty that he resented and there was nothing attractive about duty. She didn't know and quite frankly she was tired of trying to figure it out. Her head ached with the constant questions whirling around inside it.

Suddenly her patience, worn paper-thin, snapped. She was done with waiting. She cleared her throat. 'Sebastian.' Her voice, pitched low, carried.

There was a perceptible pause before Sebastian turned around long enough for her cheeks to begin to burn at the prospect of being humiliated.

An unexpected rush of anger-fuelled adrenaline kept the tears she felt burning behind her eyelids at bay.

She watched, the sinking feeling not improving as he said something that made the trio with him nod, and he began to walk towards her, his dark hair gleaming glossy blue under the light cast by the chandeliers, his scar made to appear darker by the same trick of the light.

In profile during the journey it had been hidden, but now, full face, the thin angry line on the left cheek of his lean face was revealed. The sight made her shiver as it always did, not because she found the blemish on his perfect face repulsive but because of how he had received it.

Her fault.

She straightened her spine, the reaction involuntary as he walked towards her with the long strides of someone who possessed natural athletic grace. Power refined and controlled that sent a visceral little shudder through her body.

He paused a few feet away and swept her face with his gaze. She thought she saw emotion move beneath the azure surface before his long dark lashes half lowered, making it impossible to read any further clues, and when he spoke his voice held no discernible inflection.

'You look tired.' The edge of roughness to the husky texture of his voice added depth to the velvet.

Realising after a lengthening silence that the comment hadn't been rhetorical and he expected her to respond, Sabrina tipped her head. 'Yes,' she agreed. Tired hardly came close to describing the bone-deep weariness she felt.

'You should go up.' His eyes moved beyond her and a woman appeared, as if by magic, smartly dressed in a blouse and tweed skirt. She dipped her head deferentially towards Sabrina.

'Mrs Reid will show you to your room if you need anything...? I will join you presently.'

Her liquid dark brown eyes flickered wider at the statement, alarm bleeping briefly through the horrible *flatness* of her emotions. Then it was gone and so was he, moving towards the waiting group. She could see that he had already dismissed her from his mind.

Simultaneously recognising the tightness in her chest as hurt, utterly irrational given their circumstances, she asked herself if she'd prefer he acted a part? Yes, actually she would. She was all for pretence if it stopped someone feeling wretched.

'I hope you like your rooms. His Highness usually has the West Wing suite when he stays with us. He said it would be fine.'

'What?' Sabrina paused, the light-headed feeling made her wonder if she had eaten anything today. The woman with her paused too, as had the group in the hall. Her husband was the only one *not* watching their progress.

What were they all thinking?

Were they asking themselves what sort of marriage this was where the husband needed to be reminded that his wife was there? She experienced a sudden flash of anger.

He could, with a minimum of effort, have made this day slightly less awful.

She hadn't been expecting him to serenade her or carry her over the threshold, even. But would it be *too* much to ask that he acknowledged her existence, show some degree of basic courtesy instead of behaving with the charm and charisma of an adolescent being forced to attend a family function when he would rather hang out with his friends? Of course, Sebastian was not an adolescent and the friends he probably wished he were hanging out with were six-foot blondes in tiny bikinis, but essentially the situation was the same. He was clearly, 'Sulking.'

She could almost hear her elocution teacher, the poor man who had been brought in by her parents when her first attempt at public speaking had not only brought her out in hives but been inaudible, applauding her projection.

Her stomach clenched in horror, the rest of her froze, as thanks to the excellent acoustics the angry accusation echoed once, twice, three times before fading away.

In the hall you could hear in the pin-drop silence Sebastian's voice sounding tersely impatient. 'So does anyone have the financial projections I asked for?'

In her head Sabrina could hear her mother's voice as she coaxed her out from the cupboard she had retreated to after she'd admitted to her best friend that she fancied the captain of the football team, unaware that she was standing close enough to the live mic to have the entire assembled school hear her.

'You have two choices when you make a public faux pas, Brina—you can either make a joke of it or act as though it never happened.'

Sabrina went for the latter and turned to the woman who was escorting her, comforting herself with the fact her new husband had the sort of attention span that meant unless you were six feet and blonde—and she was five six and fairish—he had pretty much deleted you from memory five seconds after you went out of his line of vision.

She lifted her chin. She would not vie for his attention but she would not be treated as though she were invisible either.

She produced a smile that said she was actually interested. 'I'm sure the rooms will be perfect, thank you. This is a beautiful house.'

She'd said the right thing. The housekeeper was very proud of her employers' historic home. She went on to regale Sabrina with a history that revolved mostly around the famous and infamous figures who had stayed there over the centuries.

CHAPTER NINE

THEY RESPONDED TO his question in a respectful way, even though they had just given the said information to him ten seconds earlier. Still, the respect was as yet only skin deep. He was perfectly well aware that he had yet to earn this. They, and in fact the world, were still waiting and maybe, in some cases, hoping that the day would come when he'd roll up for a scheduled conference late, hungover or possibly both.

Sometimes their doubts, never voiced, felt like a shout, but he knew that he could not allow self-doubt to creep in, so the extra hours he put in were not to prove anything to the doubters, but to himself.

'This could wait until the morning if you prefer, Highness,' said Ramon, the accountant.

'You have somewhere else you'd prefer to be, Ramon?'

The man adopted an expression that suggested he wanted nothing more than to discuss a report on the financial benefits to be gained from amalgamating the tourist boards of both sides of the reunified island!

'Fine, I believe there is coffee provided for us in the study.'

Sebastian could feel their resentment as they filed past him. They all had places they would prefer to be, whereas he had a place he did not want to be.

Keeping his libido on a leash around her was driving him closer to the edge on the occasions when he was unable to avoid contact, but as hard as it was, as much as he wanted her, his guilt—or was that his pride?—would not allow him to act on it.

He didn't want her *available* or *willing* or *dutiful*. Sebastian wanted her mad, crazy, hungry for him. In his dreams she begged him to come to her and he would wake up bathed in sweat and aching.

Sebastian's jaw clenched as he lost his battle not to look towards the staircase in time to see her vanish from view.

'Highness, is there anything I can get you?'

The form of address dragged Sabrina's wandering thoughts back from the dark place they had drifted to. She was barely aware that they had reached the suite of rooms that they had been allocated. The woman walked her through them, opening the doors to two en-suite bedrooms that opened off a large, comfortable central sitting room.

'Would you like a fire lit?'

Sabrina's eyes went to the fireplace. 'No, that's fine, thank you,' she murmured, waiting until the woman had left before leaning against the closed door.

She stood there, eyes closed for a few moments, before levering herself away from the surface and giving herself a mental shake before she looked around the room. Even without an audience she found herself feigning an interest she was far from feeling, a *lifetime's training kicking in*.

They were only scheduled to spend one night here but someone had gone to a lot of trouble. Or more likely an army of 'someones' had. There were the welcoming touches, like the flower arrangements, the iced champagne. Opening one of the doors that led off the sitting room, Sabrina stared at the neatly turned down four-poster that took centre stage. The bed in the second, equally grand bedroom was turned down too. Not letting her mind go there, she continued to deal with the moment and not think beyond it, preferring to deal with each situation as it arose before moving on to the next hurdle.

Hurdle—was that what her married life was going to be?

She frowned. If you started thinking of yourself as some sort of helpless victim, inevitably you became one. She turned her back on the bed and opened one of the numerous fitted cupboards that lined one wall, where she found a selection of her own clothes hanging neatly on hangers, along with a row of shoes.

It wasn't until she opened it fully and caught a glimpse of herself in the mirror-lined door that she saw she was still clutching a sad-looking bouquet in her gloved hand.

Peeling off her silk gloves, she walked back into the sitting room and sat down, loosening the top button of the blouse she wore beneath her cream silk suit. It didn't help the restricted feeling in her chest. There was still that cold, heavy weight behind her breastbone that she had spent the day pretending wasn't there.

Sitting upright again, she kicked off the heels she wore and flexed her fingers, staring as she did at the rings that felt cold, the wide gold band above the square-cut emerald engagement ring, and fought a sudden compulsion to tear them off.

The act would have been both pointless and childish and now was the moment to behave like an adult, so instead, to distract herself from the feelings that were building inside her, she reached for the TV remote, pressed the on button and began to scroll through the channels.

She closed her eyes and let her head fall back. She allowed the husky diction of a well-known female newsreader to wash over her.

The woman actually had quite a pleasant voice, soothing, until that one phrase made her jolt into a tense upright position—*Princess Sabrina*!

On the screen the newsreader's face was replaced by a scene of the wedding guests, the camera zooming in close-up on a few famous faces.

'It is believed that after being left quite literally at the altar last June by the then Crown Prince Luis, his jilted bride, Lady Sabrina Summerville, has married his brother, Prince Sebastian, at a private ceremony. The couple and the bride's sister were both involved in the tragic accident on Vela Main on the day of the wedding.'

The images of the wedding guests vanished and in their place was footage of helicopters circling and ambulances with wailing sirens, their flashing lights illuminating wreckage strewn across a road.

Sabrina stared transfixed at the nightmare scene of twisted metal and bodies, unaware as the remote slipped from her nerveless fingers.

She hoped that Chloe was not watching this.

She gave a sigh of relief as the crash scene vanished, though the tension climbed straight back into her shoulders as Sebastian appeared on the screen, tall and tanned, looking like the hero of an action movie. Over one broad shoulder he carried skis while the other shoulder was occupied by the fashionably tousled blonde head of a leggy soap actress who had both her arms around his middle as she smiled for the cameras that surrounded them. Sebastian looked down at her with an expression of amused indulgence before turning to the camera crews as he made a gesture that ensured the photo being plastered over front pages the next day.

'Sabrina…'

She leapt at the touch of his hand on her shoulder and fumbled for the remote.

'What rubbish are you watching?' he asked, sounding impatient.

'I'm not watching,' she denied, annoyed with herself for feeling inexplicably guilty, then almost immediately embarrassed as a picture of herself looking solemn with pigtails and no front teeth, one from the family album, filled the screen.

Her fingers had closed over the remote but just as she was about to press the off button Count Hugo appeared, looking sincere as he stared into the camera.

'What the…?'

Behind her Sebastian drawled, 'I think it might be a good idea to watch this.'

'You realise, Count,' said the man holding the microphone, 'that many will believe this marriage is one of political expedience? Prince Luis was a popular figure both sides of the border. Many question his brother's ability to fill his shoes, and this marriage today—this rather low-key marriage—is it not true to say that it is nothing more than a cynical stunt to shore up crumbling support for the reunification project?'

The Count, who had continued to smile benignly into the camera through the comments, remained unflustered as he posed his own question.

'Donald, I ask you, if it was a "stunt", as you call it,

would it be low-key? One can never silence the cynics, but the facts are, whether you choose to believe them or not, that the Prince and his bride have known one another for years, and have been…close in the past. After the events of last June the respect they have always felt for one another has turned into love.'

The newsreader's face appeared as the Count vanished.

'You can see the full report tomorrow night at nine, when the reunification is discussed by a panel of experts—but here is a—'

Sabrina pressed the 'off' button and turned, her expression accusing as she faced her husband.

'Did you know about this?'

'No…'

She arched a sceptical brow. She could not believe that the Count would have gone ahead with something like that without running it past Sebastian first.

'But I'm not exactly surprised, and I'm not really sure why you are.'

'You're not surprised to hear that *you're* one half of one of the greatest love stories of the decade?' She folded her arms across her chest and glared up at him. 'Well, it came as news to me.'

Sebastian reacted to the spiky sarcasm in her voice with a negligent shrug. 'The question is, did he have you convinced? I thought he came across as surprisingly sincere,' he mused, tugging off the tie that was looped around his neck.

'Does it not bother you that he was lying his head off?' she squeaked incredulously.

Sebastian gave a cynical smile. 'Yes, he was lying. He is a diplomat. It is what he does.'

'And he just goes ahead and does it? He doesn't run it past anyone?'

'He has a level of autonomy.'

She could tell that was only half the story. 'You're just as bad as he is!' she accused. But Sebastian was much better to look at. 'Is there some special class where they teach you how to dodge a question?'

'Actually, yes.' He removed his eyes from the pouting outline of her lips. 'I asked him to handle the press. I don't micromanage but I think the brief I gave him was too…broad.'

She rolled her eyes. 'Finally! And you're all right with what he did?' Her voice shook with the sense of outrage she felt.

He gave her a very direct look and a surprisingly straight answer. 'I am not happy.'

Something in the clipped delivery made her look at him. Sabrina became aware for the first time that he was actually pretty angry. She felt an unexpected stab of sympathy for the Count.

Sebastian glanced at the blank screen of the television. 'It was…tasteless. He overstepped the mark, but that's politics for you.'

She subsided with a sigh into a chair. 'I don't like politics.'

He flashed a bleak grin. 'It's not going to go away any time soon.' He walked across to the table and picked up the bottle from the ice bucket. 'You look like you need a drink.'

She shook her head automatically and wrapped her arms around herself, squeezing tight until her fingers dug into her ribcage, hard enough to bruise. Her chin rested against her chest as she closed her eyes.

'Well, I do.' He put both the champagne flutes he had filled down on the polished surface.

'Do you ever have flashbacks…?' she asked. He looked at her as she shook her head. 'It doesn't matter.'

His frown deepened. 'How do you mean flashbacks?'

'The accident.'

'Do you?'

'It's got better. The therapist said—'

'You have seen a therapist?'

'My parents insisted.'

'Does anyone else know this?'

'Anyone?' she countered, her brow pleating into a puzzled frown.

'Anyone other than your parents?' he pressed. 'Did you discuss it with friends or—?'

Her sudden shocked laugh cut him off. 'You think there is some sort of *stigma* attached to having counselling for post-traumatic stress?'

'What I think is not relevant.'

She felt her anger and, yes, disappointment, swell a tight knot in her chest. 'Actually I think it's *very* relevant.'

'In our position it pays to be aware, anticipate the effect our actions will have. We must always be conscious of how the public perceive them. From this point on our lives, everything we do, is going to be scrutinised.'

'What do you mean,' she asked, 'from this point on? You have spent your life playing for the cameras.'

Spasms of irritation flickered across his face. 'Mental health is a sensitive issue and the press can spin—'

'You're afraid that people will say you've married someone unstable? You know something, Sebastian? I actually don't care what you think,' she shouted. How much simpler her life would be if that were true! 'I had a problem. I couldn't sleep and I got help.' She drew a slicing motion with her hand. 'End of story.'

'Don't overreact!'

His dismissive attitude made her jaw quiver. 'I'm not the one overreacting. You can't deal with it—*tough*, Sebastian! But you know what I think? *You're* the one with the problem,' she charged, her brown eyes sparking with contemptuous accusation.

He watched, jaw clenched, his anger slipping away as Sabrina bent and picked up the slingback heels she had been wearing, pulling the silk across her deliciously rounded bottom tight before she straightened up and flung him a look of contempt over her shoulder. Then, shoes dangling from the fingers of one hand, her slender back rigid, she flounced in a dignified fashion from the room.

He winced at the sound of the door slamming.

Eyes squeezed closed, he lifted one of the glasses he had filled to his lips. The fizz slid smoothly down his throat but didn't produce any lightening of his mood as the bubbles seeped into his bloodstream.

With a curse he slammed the glass down, before he began to pace across the room. He was furious with her for being unforgivably right. He exhaled, his chest lifting as he came to a halt, eyes closed, a low grunt of self-directed anger rumbling in his chest.

She was right and he had never felt more ashamed of himself. What the hell was wrong with him? He had responded to her confidence like the sort of narrow-minded bigot he despised. She wouldn't be doing any confiding in him again in a hurry.

Maybe that was why he'd done it, as another way to push her away?

How many times had he sneered when his father had

adopted a similar attitude? Truth was disposable; unfairness could always be spun in your favour.

After a moment he walked towards the recently closed door.

The room was empty. One lamp beside the bed was switched on, illuminating the darkness. He could hear the sound of running water in the bathroom. Calling Sabrina's name, he walked across the room. The bathroom door was open and she stood barefooted in a silk slip at the marble washbasin, her hands under the running tap as she stared at her reflection in the mirror.

'Sabrina.'

She reacted to the sound of her name like a startled deer and spun around, wary-eyed, to face him. Their eyes connected and her chin lifted to a haughty angle, despite the blue-veined pulse he could see leaping at the base of her creamy throat. 'Do you mind knocking before you come into my room?'

'Yes, as a matter of fact I do, and I'm damned if I'm going to start off this marriage with sulks and closed doors.'

She switched off the water and stalked past him. 'Fine, next time I'll lock it. And I'm not sulking.'

'I'm sorry…'

She had been ready to counter anything he threw at her except that…an apology! It crossed her mind she had misheard him. 'What did you say?'

'I'm sorry. That was…' He hefted a sigh and dragged a hand back and forth across his already mussed hair. 'I'm so busy pretending to be the Prince everyone wants that it's hard to switch off.'

That was the way he operated. He focused on the task at hand. It had never mattered what the task was; he gave all the same commitment and he didn't carry baggage to weigh him down. Because he had shrugged off the accident it had not even crossed his mind to consider that it might not be so easy for Sabrina.

Her dark eyes widened. 'You don't have to prove anything to anyone.'

He shrugged, an ironic half-smile quivering the corners of his mouth. 'Only myself maybe. You must be aware that people are waiting for me to fail?'

She shifted uneasily, feeling an unexpected stab of sympathy for Sebastian as she remembered the comments earlier that day of his father's aide.

Her fingers playing with the thin spaghetti strap of her silk slip drew his eyes to the smooth curve of her shoulder.

'Well, you have worked pretty hard at establishing yourself as the Playboy Prince, haven't you?'

He gave a hard grin, the gleam in his blue eyes and the flash of white teeth making her stomach flip. 'That was not all hard work—some of it came naturally. Look, I am not going to pretend I am something I am not. I am not a romantic…which, considering our circumstances, might not in itself be a drawback. I was never looking for a soulmate—'

'Or a wife.'

He blinked; she could see that her comment had caught him unawares. 'True, but marriage is a contract and I understand contracts.'

But not love.

Sebastian didn't believe in love and maybe that made it easier than believing in it as she did, and knowing that it was something she could never have.

Don't think about the things you can't have, Brina, she told herself. *Focus on the things you can have, the things you can achieve…you can have children…* Something she had always considered one of the greatest gifts a woman could be blessed with. Beyond that she had allowed herself to believe that she might be in a position one day to have influence on things she cared about: health care, women's education... She might be able to leave a legacy even if she could not have love.

'People aren't always looking. Luis wasn't looking and he found his soulmate.'

'I am not Luis, Sabrina.'

'No, you didn't run, but you wanted to!' she countered, knowing the accusation was unfair but unable to repress the great sense of frustration she felt.

'I am not a romantic. I do not believe that I will be walking down a street and be struck by the emotional version of a lightning bolt when I find my soulmate. You regret that you have not had your time out there kissing frogs and waiting for one to turn into a prince. The fact is, the only Prince you will have is me...but I promise you, *cara*,' he continued, his voice softening to a low, throaty, toe-curling purr as he took another step towards her, 'those butterflies you spoke of do not require a soulmate. You can feel them. You *will* feel them.'

Heart racing, her blood pounding, she quivered but didn't evade his hand as his fingers trailed down her cheek, the light touch sparking nerve endings to life before his hand fell away.

'You sound very confident.'

'There has been an attraction between us from the first moment we met. I really don't want our married life to start with closed doors. How about we push those doors open?'

Their eyes locked, neither spoke; the touch of his hand on the bare skin of her shoulder made her jump.

She moved to pull the strap of her slip up but his free hand caught her wrist.

Her heart was thudding a wild drumbeat in her chest as her glance moved from the fingers circling her wrist to his big hand, brown against her skin. She swallowed and looked back up into the burning blue of his eyes and she felt her resistance slipping away like sand through her fingers.

She managed a sensible smile, hard when he was close, so impossibly male. 'Sebastian, this is not a good—'

His grin sizzled away her sensible thoughts.

'To hell with good!' he growled throatily, then, still holding her gaze, he let go of her hand and took hold of the hem of her slip, which he pulled over her head in one slick motion.

She didn't move.

The sexual tension had reached screaming point in one slam of a heartbeat.

His hands followed the path of his eyes as they slid down her neck, over her shoulders then down to her quivering breasts. His fingers splaying to cup them, as his thumbs teased the hot, aching peaks.

Her eyes squeezed tight shut as she stood, head back, hands clenched into white-knuckled fists as she focused on the incredible sensations coursing through her body, opening only when he spread his hands under her rib-cage around her waist.

He bent his head and covered her mouth, the kiss slow and sensual. She could see the sensuous glitter in his eyes through the screen of his long lashes. When he pulled back, desire, hot and fierce, roared inside her.

He rubbed his nose up against hers, blowing wisps of

hair from her eyes before he moved in again. This time the kisses were not slow, they were hard and hungry.

Still kissing her on her lips, her neck, her eyes… everywhere, he picked her up and carried her over to the bed. Lying there, she watched as he stripped, holding her eyes as he fought his way out of his clothes, revealing a lean and muscled body, his golden skin dusted with strategic drifts of dusky hair.

And he was really, really aroused.

The image of primitive male beauty sent a fresh surge of breathless excitement through Sabrina's body. One hand on the mattress beside her, he bent forward. Greedy, she looped her arms around his neck and dragged him down onto the bed beside her.

The first skin-to-skin contact drew a shocked cry of pleasure from her throat. His skin was like silk, his body hard, the lean strength of it different and intensely thrilling.

His hands moved in long sweeping movements down her sides, her quivering thighs, before moving to her bottom. He kneaded the tight flesh with his fingers, dragging her in hard against his body as she pushed up and into him, opening her mouth to the invasion of his tongue. Wanting to open herself to him so much at one level it scared her, but the fear was lost in the need; the deep, driving, relentless throb of need that had invaded every cell of her body.

'Hell, Sabrina!' he breathed against her mouth.

'Hell, back,' she teased, kissing the scar on his face, letting her tongue run down the length of it before framing his face between her small hands and saying fiercely, 'I hated you hurting.'

He groaned. He was hurting now!

Was it always like this, or was this hot make-up sex?

he wondered as he slid down her body. His thought processes stopped as he fitted his mouth hungrily to one perfect tight nipple and felt her moan and arch under him.

He tipped her over, sliding up her body until they were lying side by side. Her skin was hot to the touch and felt like silk…he couldn't believe how soft.

'Incredible,' he murmured as he slid a hand down behind her knee and hooked her leg across his hip. She bent her head and pressed her face into his chest, kissing the hair-roughened skin.

He slid his fingers into her hair and dragged her face up to his, then he slid a hand between her legs, his fingers moving through the light curls into her body.

Sabrina ached for his touch. There was nothing outside the ache; it consumed her totally, hit everywhere she moved against his hand, her breath coming in a series of uneven, shallow little gasps as his fingers slid along her delicate folds and deep into her.

Quite suddenly he rolled away and lay on his back, gasping like a man coming up for air. He turned his head and looked at her. 'I can't take much more of this.'

She gave a slow, slumberous smile, the primal need pounding through her making her bold, as she placed her hand in the middle of his chest, watching his face as she moved her hand lower.

She watched him gasp as her fingers tightened slowly around him.

He withstood the torture for a few seconds until his control broke. With a low growl that rose up from some place deep inside him, he tipped her onto her back and parted her legs and positioned himself between them. He watched her face as he thrust slowly, deeply into her.

Then deeper, as he begged her to take him all and she

wrapped her long legs around him and closed her eyes, whispering his name over and over like a litany as they moved together, breath mingled, touching everywhere, heartbeats in sync, as close as two people could be.

She felt it coming, she pushed towards it, every muscle in her body tensed and waiting, and when the white-hot rush came it was so strong it pushed her to the edge of consciousness.

When she fought her way back from the blissful place he had taken her to Sebastian was still lying across her, breathing hard, then with a groan he levered himself off her.

'I was rough… Should I say sorry?'

She touched a finger to his lips.

He looked into her lovely face and felt a swell of possessive tenderness.

'It was perfect, you were…' She caught his hand, her eyes flickering down his lean, muscled form, before lifting it to her lips. 'I suppose practice really does make perfect.'

It wasn't until Sabrina spoke that he realised tonight was not something he had ever *practised* for; what they had shared had been nothing like anything he had *ever* experienced before. He could not compare like with like because there was no like.

'Stay?' she slurred sleepily, her eyelids flickering but not opening. It was fine by him. Sebastian could barely keep his eyes open anyway.

He slid down and drew her into his body. She settled there with the trust of a kitten and gave a gentle sigh.

CHAPTER TEN

THE DAWN CHORUS was singing when he opened his eyes and Sabrina was still in his arms, her soft body warm, face pressed against his chest. Her hair, lying in a honey-eyed stream down her slender back, was tangled.

The corners of his mouth lifted in a smile as he experienced a swelling surge of possessiveness that was outside his experience and a million miles from his objectivity. His smile flattened and then reasserted itself as she gave a little sigh and burrowed deeper into his chest. He didn't want to recognise the tenderness that tightened in his chest as he thought about last night; the sex had been mind-blowing. His eyes darkened as he remembered the moment she had taken the initiative, tentative at first as she'd begun to explore his body with her hands and mouth, and then with more confidence as she'd learned to drive him to the brink and bring him back. Her instincts were incredible, her lack of inhibitions a delight.

It was just sex. So why, asked the voice in his head, had it felt like no sex he had ever known? Did a marriage licence really make such a difference? He had never been a woman's first before—maybe that was part of it. The fact that everything was new and fresh for her and her delight and wonder…her *hunger* made it new and fresh for him.

He lifted a strand of hair from her face and leaned in, breathing in the scent of her warm skin until the ringing phone in the other room reminded him that this respite had been temporary.

He eased his arm slowly from under her shoulders, and, pulling the sheet up over her naked body, he slipped from the bed. On his way to the door he grabbed one of the bathrobes that were hung up and closed the door quietly behind him. The phone had stopped ringing and it took him a couple of minutes to locate it to where it had slipped from his pocket. A glance at the screen revealed the identity of the person behind the five missed calls.

With a sigh he punched in the number. 'Hello, Father.'

Sabrina fought her way through several layers of wispy sleep before she surfaced, not quite sure where she was or why she ached in muscles that she didn't know she had.

She opened her eyes and encountered the cobalt-blue stare of the man who was standing at the foot of the bed sipping coffee.

Her husband!

Her lover!

She cut short her sinuous little stretch, sucked in a taut breath and sat up, dragging the sheet with her.

'What time is it?'

'Early.'

'You're…' *Not naked,* she thought, taking in his suit and feeling a little stab of disappointment.

'A meeting scheduled for tomorrow has been brought forward.'

'What meeting?'

He looked surprised by the question. 'The geological team who did the new survey are available to answer some questions. I have to fly back.'

She blinked, her brain still not working at full capacity. 'How long do I have to get ready?'

'No need for that. Take your time. I'm flying out.'

A cold, resentful feeling in the pit of her stomach expanded. She focused on that and not the hurt. 'Without me.'

'You are not missing much, I promise.' He put down his coffee cup and got to his feet. 'Depending on when the meeting ends, we will meet up tonight.'

Was that shorthand for *to have sex*? She didn't know, but she was concerned by how much she wanted it to be. Hell, one night and she was already an addict! It was no longer a surprise to her that her husband had left a swathe of broken hearts across Europe.

'Last night I…' She paused, unable to find the words to tell him how *right* it had felt without sounding…*besotted*.

'We are expected to make a baby or two. I think we might enjoy it.'

She brought her lashes down in a concealing sweep. It wasn't what he'd said, it was the realisation that she had wanted him to say something *more*, to *feel* something more.

Because she felt more, Sabrina realised, she *wanted* more, she…oh, hell, she had fallen in love with her Playboy Prince, but he was so much more. Pain and shock seeped through her, because for him she would always be a duty, even if it was one he enjoyed. At least when the lights were out and no others duties demanded his attention.

She was his wife but not his love.

'Are you all right?'

She dodged his eyes and pulled the sheet all the way up to her chin. Was this what being in love felt like? Nerve endings raw and exposed? The stomach churning? The need to cry until your eyes were red and puffy?

If so she was amazed it was so popular, that people actively looked for it. She'd had flu that felt better than being in love.

'Fine.'

Sabrina was a very bad liar, but, rather than challenge the very obvious untruth, Sebastian accepted the statement at face value with a shrug of his muscled shoulders because— *Because it's easier and you're a coward, Seb.*

'I'm not really human until I've had my first coffee.'

The brightness in her voice sent a knife surge of guilt through him as he lowered his lean frame onto the edge of the bed. 'I know.'

Eyes dark, wide and wary lifted very slowly to his face as she began to shake her head. 'No, it isn't…'

'You're dreading moving into your golden cage… I do understand.'

Her dark lashes came down in a fluttering curtain across her eyes; she gave something that sounded like a laugh before raising them again.

'Palace life is restricting, but…' He took a deep breath. It didn't matter how many times he told himself she knew what she was letting herself in for, that they were *both* victims of this situation, he still felt guilty as hell. 'Our apartments will be separate from my father and you…*we*…must…'

'Make the best of a bad job. Keep busy,' she quipped with a brittle smile as he danced around the message he was delivering: that their lives might collide and sometimes in the bedroom, but essentially they were to live their own lives. It was nothing more than she had ever expected from marriage, but that had been before she had been stupid enough to fall in love with her husband.

That changed everything!

'That wasn't what I was going to say. The next twelve months…the workload will be… I won't be there to—'

She lifted her chin, her pride coming to her rescue. 'I am not a child, Sebastian, so relax. I do not need entertaining.'

I just need loving!

'I do not need my hand held,' she continued, ignoring the ache in her chest. 'And I am not going to be a *needy* wife,' she promised, managing to inject a note of amusement into her voice. 'I'm not going to ask you for anything.'

She finished saying what he wanted to hear, getting a hard look for her efforts.

Sebastian knew he should be feeling relief; instead he felt an odd sense of dissatisfaction as he listened to her list the things she would *not* be asking of him. He knew that anger was an irrational response but struggled to put his finger on the exact cause.

'What if I need my hand holding?' From her expression the unplanned question appeared to surprise her almost as much as it had him. 'Not literally, just a figure of speech,' he said, responding to a need to clarify his comment. After all, he had never actually needed someone…anyone.

The addition made her wonder if she had imagined the hard-sounding question. Her eyes flickered from the brown hand he had moved across the counterpane until his splayed fingertips were a whisper away from her own, before shifting back to his face. A wave of sheer longing and lust pierced her like a knife blade, causing her chest to lift as she caught her breath.

'Oh, for one moment there I thought the story that you don't actually need more than one hour's sleep a night was more than an urban myth.'

He responded with a half-smile to her comeback, not seeming to notice her heightened colour. 'I have watched your parents. They work as a team.'

She nodded agreement. 'Yes, but that's different. They—'

'Love one another.'

It wasn't his assertion that sparked her angry response but the patronising little half-smile that accompanied it, though that faded as he continued. 'But leaving the emotional stuff to one side…'

Suddenly the anger blocked out everything. It was simply too extreme for her to navigate around. 'As far as I'm concerned marriage…a *real* marriage…is all about the *emotional stuff*! There,' she charged, discovering that it was possible to love someone and want to throw something at them at one and the same time. 'Is *that* emotional enough for you? Sorry if I lack your control!'

The mattress shifted, making her slide sideways as he got to his feet and turned, spreading his hands in a pacifying gesture as he looked down at her. 'I'm sorry if I'm throwing the cold water of realism on your dreams, but we have to be realistic. Palace life…marriage, if I can say the word without you throwing something at me? It will take some adjusting to but things might work better if we don't immediately form two opposing camps, if we are one…team.'

His logic was impeccable and deeply depressing, and the only thing, she reminded herself, on offer.

She lifted her brows before directing her retort at her pearly polished toenails. 'Who knows? Your robot logic might cancel out my silly, girly emotionalism.' As the last quivering resentful words left her lips her head lifted, but there was no answering anger in Sebastian's face as their eyes clashed. He looked…hell, he looked incredibly sexy and *exhausted*. Her anger was lost in a wave of protective empathy.

'For God's sake, Sabrina, I want you in my bed, not in my head!' he blasted, then saw her expression and stopped, a curse of frustration escaping his clenched teeth. 'Sorry, I didn't mean—'

'Yes, you did.' She sat there looking frozen, offended and so incredibly sexy with her honey tumbled hair and pink mouth still partly swollen from their kisses from the previous night that he experienced the tsunami of all hormone surges. It struck with no warning and the results on his brain function was devastating—a white-hot, brain-melting blast.

Endurance was the only response. Waiting for it to pass, Sebastian closed his eyes, the muscles of his throat working as he fought for control—this should not be happening. Sex should have smoothed the path; the absence of love should have meant this was easier, not more complicated…yet another occasion when theory fell well short of reality!

He took a deep breath and tried again to breach the chasm he could feel forming between them. 'Look…' Their eyes connected and the silence stretched, only interrupted by the discordant sounds of their individual jagged breathing.

'Marriage does not have to conform to any set pat-

tern. We need to set out our own rules, not conform…
and we must be flexible.' She had been beautifully flexible last night.

'What are you saying?' she whispered, unable to
tear her eyes away from his hot, scorching stare. Her
insides were melting.

Good question, he thought. 'I really don't know…'
he said, because this was very much outside his experience. 'I can't promise anything, Sabrina. I know you
have dreams and…' He gave a short laugh, hating himself and the system for all that she had been robbed of.
'Maybe you never had any, but anyway I'm sorry that
this is your life, the politics, the scheming. I guess what
I'm trying to say is that I don't want us to be warring
factions, sending notes to one another through a third
party. You deserve more than that.' *And more than me,*
he thought.

His driven words penetrated the warm sexual whirl-
pool that was drawing her inside, a weird but oddly
seductive experience. 'That won't happen,' she managed faintly.

'It could. I've seen it in action…my parents…no
matter what, we will never be them.' *Kill me first,* he
thought. 'I'd tell you about it but maybe in the long run
it will just get easier when this chemistry wears off.'

Did the fact his deep voice was actually shaking
with need make his prediction any the less painful?
The rampant hunger glowing in his eyes made this a
question for later; right now all she wanted to do was
feel him inside her.

'But in the meantime let's enjoy it?' he growled.

The hungry intent stamped on his lean face made
her insides quiver with helpless desire.

Sebastian was fighting his way out of his jacket as he levered his long length onto the bed beside her.

Sabrina helped him.

It was the following day before he saw her next.

In that time, he had been able to gain some perspective, and a little sympathy he had previously lacked for people who actually convinced themselves that a hormonal response was something spiritual and everlasting. It was an easy mistake to make, he now appreciated.

Of course, there was more involved with his situation with Sabrina. They were two people in a unique arrangement that very few would ever experience; the affinity, the sense of understanding, when combined with a physical attraction had, when you viewed the situation logically, been almost predictable.

Then he saw her, and the smug, comforting conclusions slipped through his fingers like sand.

'Hello, there.'

Sabrina started guiltily, looking from him to the heavy tome in her lap. She removed the rather sexy specs that had been balanced on the end of her nose.

'Sorry!' she said as she stood, clutching the heavy book to her chest. 'We weren't expecting you until later.'

'Is that a royal we?'

She tried to slide her foot back into a sandal. 'Hard to be royal when you're barefoot.' Hard to sound as if you had more than one brain cell when this man was standing so close. 'How did it go?'

Well done, Brina, you sounded almost sane and not sadly deluded and desperately in love.

He dragged a hand through his hair 'I have some sympathy with the idea of being a despot…'

'That's because you are incredibly impatient.' Gifted with a quick mind and an exceptional intellect, Sebastian struggled, she suspected, with the intellectual pace of a normal human being.

'So what are you reading?'

Heart beating fast, she hugged the book closer to her chest, knowing she looked guilty as she shrugged and took a step back. 'Just a thing…nothing really.'

He bent down to her level and read the spine, running a finger along it as he read out the title. '"*Dementia and the Socio-Economic Impact on Developing Nations…*" Wow, racy stuff! Don't look so worried—it can be our guilty secret.'

'Someone I know wrote it. They asked me for a review.'

'So they are getting paid to read it?'

She frowned, wondering if that was against the rules. 'Not exactly. I keep the book.'

His teasing smile faded as the full impact of what she had left behind, the expertise that she was never likely to use, hit home. In contrast to the knot of anger in his belly, his voice was gentle. 'This really is not your world, is it?'

'It is now.' She lifted her chin and along with it any wimpish impulses to throw herself at him and confess it had been awful: the arrival, tea with the Queen and being introduced to the women who she was expected to be friends with, *suitable* women.

She could deal with that, but she would be the wife he needed even if he didn't know he needed her yet… *Would he ever?* 'You never said—beyond discovering buried despotic tendencies you discovered, how was your day?'

Better since I saw you.

And the shocks just kept coming, he thought, pressing a hand to the region of his chest where the pleasurable warmth had ignited when he'd seen her sitting with her bare feet dangling in the historic fountain. He lowered his hand and focused instead on the lust that had come with it. There was something delightfully uncomplicated about lust. It was one of the basic needs in life, like hunger and sleep, and he was tired. It was a known fact that exhaustion could do weird things to a man's brain.

His glance slid to the inches of smooth calf revealed as she lifted her skirt to grimace at the inches of damp silk that clung to those smooth calves. As it lifted he saw there was still a question in her eyes.

'Long.' And so were her legs.

The signs of tiredness in his face intensified the ache inside her.

'And you?'

'I had tea with your…the Queen.'

'And you're not lying down in a darkened room? I'm impressed.'

'She was trying to be helpful.'

One dark brow elevated. 'That bad.'

'Apparently I am meeting a stylist tomorrow.'

'No!'

Her eyes flew up to his face. 'No what?'

'Just no, you do not need a *stylist*, and the last thing you need is to be turned into some sort of "ladies who lunch" clone, and the idea that you need a makeover is an insult.'

His indignation on her behalf made her lips twitch but also filled her with a deep sense of relief. She didn't want to emulate the women she had met today. 'Is that an executive decision?'

He arched a haughty brow. 'You have a problem with that?'

She gave a tiny smile. 'I'll let you know when I have a problem.' She responded to the touch of his hand on her elbow, skipping a little to keep up with his long-legged pace. 'Obviously I can't offend the Queen.'

He gave a laugh. 'She has the hide of a rhino.'

'I will see the stylist.'

He stopped and swung her around to face him.

'I'll just ignore what he says.'

The annoyance slowly faded from his face and he laughed.

'It's called diplomacy, Seb. You should try it.'

He placed his hands on her shoulders and leaned in closer, his breath warm on the cool skin of her face. 'You offering to give me lessons, *cara*?'

She shivered and raised herself onto her toes and his mouth brushed across her wavering lips. 'Sometimes,' she whispered, 'the direct approach is better.'

She went limp as the hunger in his kiss drove the breath from her body.

He stroked her face and felt the tensions of the day slip away. 'You really are a very beautiful woman, Sabrina.' She sighed and turned her face into his hand. 'I've never believed that it is possible to maintain any sort of friendship with a woman after an affair is over, but we just might.'

Her half-closed eyes snapped open and she stepped back abruptly, leaving him holding empty air. What the hell had just happened?

'What's wrong?'

She gave an inarticulate little growl of fury and stuck out her chin, glaring at him, dark eyes glowing with angry contempt as the words fell from her lips in an angry rush. His comment had pierced the protective shell of a core of pain she hadn't known was there until now.

'That you have to ask that says it all! I'm not a woman you're having an affair with. I'm your wife.' In the act of turning her back on him she swung back and shook her head. 'Has it ever occurred to you that you were never friends with those women afterwards because you were never friends before?'

An expression of seething frustration on his face, he watched her stalk away, her head high, her narrow back eloquently rigid. Any inclination he had to follow her faded when she stopped twenty feet or so away and paused to fling over her shoulder, 'And, for the record, neither are we!'

CHAPTER ELEVEN

UNREASONABLE DIDN'T EVEN begin to cover her attitude, he decided as he paced up and down his study, pausing only to take a mouthful of the brandy that he held.

He had held out hope for the future and she had thrown it back in his face; she had acted as though he had insulted her!

And hadn't he?

Pushing away the suggestion, he nursed his sense of injustice along with the brandy as the level of one rose higher, the other sank lower, until the glass was empty.

He stopped pacing and sat staring morosely at the wall; as the minutes ticked away his anger slipped away. When there was a knock on the door, it opened before he responded.

Sabrina took a deep breath. It had taken her half an hour to work up the courage to do this. Half an hour after a lot of angry tears to reach the point where she had asked herself *why* she was angry.

She was angry because the future he saw, even the best-scenario future, was not the one she dreamed of. She couldn't force him to love her and she couldn't punch him for not loving her.

Rather than be angry and bitter about what she

couldn't have, she should do what he had said and enjoy what they did have while it lasted.

'I overreacted. Sebastian, I don't want to sleep alone.'

She held her breath as he got to his feet. It seemed to take a long time and even longer for him to cross the room to her.

'Neither do I.' With a groan he dragged her to him, kissing her with a rough, hungry intensity that drove the breath from her lungs and the strength from her legs. As her knees sagged he picked her up and carried her over to the sofa.

She knew it was only sex he was giving her but when she closed her eyes his tender response felt like love. When he moved inside her it felt as though they were truly one, not just physically, but in every way.

He took her to a place within herself that she hadn't known existed; she lost a sense of where she began and he ended. The sadness, deep and profound, came afterwards, when he held her tenderly, because she knew that Sebastian was not feeling what she did. He gave her his body but she would never touch his soul.

'The ladies are in the Small Salon.'

Sabrina smiled in response to the gentle reminder from her assistant and thought, *I can't wait,* but carried on moving papers around her desk.

She stopped and asked herself for the first time that day—*what am I doing?*

Beyond the obvious, which was waiting for Sebastian to return. They had spent an entire week together before he had left for a week.

She had tried to fill the hours, telling herself that she had to build a life that didn't revolve around a husband who most likely forgot she existed the moment he walked out of the room, and one day in the future when she was in the room.

Live in the moment, Brina!

Great advice, but really tough to follow through with.

Work of a sort had saved her: the timing of the approach from the university hospital, asking her to help to fill the vacancy for a head of the new Alzheimer's research unit they were keen to establish, had been perfect.

As well as using her contacts in London to line up someone for the post, Sabrina had surreptitiously channelled some funding their way too and acted suitably surprised when the dean of the faculty had remarked on their good fortune.

'The ladies?'

Sabrina, who realised she had been sitting there with her eyes closed, opened them and looked from the pencil she had just snapped in half to her assistant. She painted on a smile.

'Oh, yes, the *ladies*. And I use the term loosely.'

Rachel struggled to hide her smile.

Sabrina paused outside the open door of the room where her new *friends* were gathered and glanced in the mirror, smoothing down her already smooth hair.

The half a dozen women inside apparently represented the cream of society. One lunch had conformed her suspicions that she had nothing whatever in common with them and she despised them almost as much as she knew they despised her.

'I heard that he was seen going into her hotel suite at one in the morning.'

The low murmur of laughter made Sabrina pause in the act of entering the salon.

'Do you suppose *she* knows?'

Sabrina pressed a hand to her stomach and told herself to breathe.

'Why would she care?'

She had no problem placing this speaker with a face. Sabrina could imagine the malice and contempt in the pale eyes as the woman gave a dramatic pause before concluding, 'She's got *exactly* what she wanted…a crown.'

A *crown*…the irony drew a tiny grunt of reaction from the listening Sabrina. She smoothed a hand across the fair hair twisted away from her face in a shiny chignon, almost feeling the symbolic weight.

'And I suppose all royals are trained from birth to turn a blind eye.'

'*Royal?* Have you seen where they live? Her mother wore the same outfit to three state events last year and her father sits in the public park playing chess with the…the peasants…'

Sabrina walked quietly into the room; unobserved, she stood in the doorway and made the decision not to waste another moment of her life playing nice with these spiteful women. It came as a relief.

'Well, I feel sorry for her. If my husband cheated on *me*—'

'You don't have a husband, and if you carry on stuffing your face with pastries you won't.'

Sabrina didn't slow or quicken her pace as she walked towards the group of expensively dressed, beautifully made up women sitting around a table set for tea.

They got to their feet almost as one when they saw her.

She ignored their furtive expressions—a couple even

had not lost the ability to blush—and kept her eyes fixed on the one woman who had remained seated.

Brought up in a much more relaxed atmosphere, Sabrina had always viewed the protocol that made everyone scramble to their feet when she walked into a room ludicrous, but on this occasion?

Sabrina's smile was practised and smooth when a few moments later the other woman got to her feet, her pouty mouth twisted into a forced, rigid smile.

Sabrina's eyes moved past her to the other women. 'Please, ladies, as you were. I'm so sorry to keep you waiting but something unexpected has come up, so I'll see you all on Thursday. No, actually, no, I don't think I will. Our little gatherings are cancelled for the foreseeable future.'

She took a step towards the door before pausing and twisting back. 'Actually, we don't have *peasants*. My father was a chess grand master at seventeen, and my mother always taught me to judge the person and not the clothes they wear. Oh, and by the way, the only woman sharing my husband's bed is *me*.'

Without waiting to observe the effect of her words she swept from the room.

Her painted-on smile faded the instant she stepped out of the room. She still felt dizzy with the anger that cooled slightly as she made her way back to her office.

'Rachel, would you cancel all the lunches with the—?' She stopped as she saw the personal items that her assistant was pushing into a large tote bag. 'What are you doing? Have you been crying?' She went over and put her arm around the girl's shoulder. 'What's wrong?'

'I… I'm leaving…'

Sabrina shook her head. 'I don't understand.'

The girl managed a watery smile. 'I have been—'

'Rachel has been reassigned, Highness.'

Sabrina turned and saw a tall woman whose presence she had not been aware of move away from the wall. She arched a brow and kept her arm around Rachel's shoulders. 'And you would be…?'

'I am Regina Cordoba, Highness—your new assistant.'

Sebastian's jaw clenched in frustration as his father's attack dog, Count Hugo, appeared from a doorway just as he was about to enter the private wing of the palace he shared with Sabrina. The man's ingratiating manner irritated him, as did his conspiracy theorist determination to blame everything that was wrong with the country on the republicans he saw lurking in every corner.

'Highness.'

Sebastian tipped his head, a glint of anger in his eyes as he responded smoothly, 'Count, lucky coincidence or—?'

'When he heard you had abandoned the meeting…?'

Sebastian arched a brow and let the silence stretch until the man, finally realising that the Prince was not about to issue an explanation, continued.

'The King hoped that you might be available, unless you are unwell?'

'Unwell?' He shook his head. The man would probably disagree if he told him why he had wound down the meeting. 'No, just…' He shook his head. 'Forget it—where is he?'

His father was in his study sitting behind his big desk that was raised on a dais. The tactic drew a wry smile from Sebastian as he walked past the chair meant for him on the lower level and straight up to the desk, where he remained standing.

'I understand you wanted to chat, Father?'

'*Chat?* I do not want to *chat*. I want an explanation as to why you saw fit to walk out of a meeting wasting the time of the people who had made the journey there.'

'Do you really want to know? Fine, well, apart from the fact that everyone was so busy protecting their own interests that we could have sat there until next week and been no further forward, I made a joke and no one laughed.'

His father stared at him.

'I know it sounds stupid but it was a very good joke and Sabrina would have got it, she would have laughed, so I came home to share it with her.' He did not add that during the absence of laughter he had strongly felt the absence of other things…or another person, and in the process had finally diagnosed the vague symptoms that had been plaguing him recently—*loneliness*… That shock had barely penetrated before he had realised that his exile from the one person who eased that ache was self-imposed.

His father, very red-faced, drew himself up in his seat. 'Well, if you are not going to do me the courtesy of being serious I can see there is no point… However, as you introduced the subject, there is something I must tell you concerning your wife.'

The faint air of humour in Sebastian's manner vanished as he laid his hand flat on the desk and leaned forward, looking at his father through narrowed eyes. 'Really?' he said with deceptive calm.

'I do not blame her—she doesn't know how we do things here—however, it has come to my attention that she has been getting involved with areas of life that are unsuitable. Like, for example, the university.'

'That well-known den of iniquity? What puzzles me is how you come to know what my wife does.'

'There are dangers, a very real threat from malcontents and terrorists. The surveillance is for protection.'

'I can and *will* protect my wife.' A smile curved his lips as he repeated the last two words 'My wife. And you will remove your spies from my meetings.'

The King blinked and looked horrified. 'I need to know—'

'And you will. I will keep you in the loop. That is the way it is and if you don't feel able to agree with my terms—'

'Terms!' The outraged King looked like a man who had just had the rug pulled out from under his feet.

'Crude, but accurate. I will do things my way or not at all and the next time I see that worm Hugo I will kick his bony butt…' His voice lowered another icy note as he straightened to his full imposing height and looked down at his father with icy contempt. 'I will do my duty by you but I will do it my way and with my wife by my side.'

'And if your wife found out about your Paris trip? There was no meeting, was there?'

'Is that a threat? Are you trying to blackmail me?'

The older man lowered his eyes. 'No, of course not, the idea is disgusting. I am your father!'

'Be careful, Father, the "how dare you?" attitude looks remarkably like guilt.'

'Me, guilty? I'm not the one spending time with—'

'My brother,' Sebastian cut in softly.

The words stopped the King dead.

Sebastian closed his eyes and cursed softly. 'I didn't mean to tell you like that. Are you all right?'

'You saw your brother?'

Sebastian nodded, feeling a spasm of pity for the old man.

'Yes, I have been in contact with Luis. We did meet up in Paris last weekend, where I met his wife, who is actually rather charming.'

'I told you I do not want that name mentioned!' the older man thundered.

'It's kind of hard to discuss the elephant in the room without saying the word elephant,' Sebastian observed. 'If you want to blank your son that is, of course, your choice—but Luis is my brother and I intend to carry on seeing him. I would like to invite him to the official reunification ceremony next year. I think he'd like to come but he has made it clear that it will only happen if the invitation comes with your blessing.'

'Never!'

Sympathy flickered into Sebastian's eyes as he got up and walked across to his father. 'You are the one who taught me the value of family.'

'He was the one who walked away. He betrayed us.'

'He fell in love.'

'Love!' his father pronounced with scorn.

'Yes, the thing that makes the world go around,' he said, picturing a pair of beautiful brown eyes. 'Luis is family, his wife is family—their child will be family.'

His father paled. 'She is pregnant?'

'It's a boy, apparently.'

He saw his father fight off a smile. 'A boy? I was beginning to think I'd never have a grandchild.'

'I am doing my best, Father.' The image of Sabrina with a child at her breast came into his head. Fatherhood was not something he had ever thought about before, except in the abstract. He was shocked by the wave of emotion that came with the image in his head.

The King cleared his throat. 'So when is this baby due?'

With a sigh Sebastian took a seat. He took a photo from his wallet and put it on the desk in front of his father. After a moment the older man took it, and when he eventually glanced down at it he stared, his eyes filling with tears.

'By the way, did I mention that the university have shown an interest in recruiting Sabrina?'

The monarch's eyes lifted. 'Just thought you'd slip that one in, did you? Raising money or even a place on the board is one thing, but your wife cannot work. That is preposterous.'

'What would be preposterous, Father, would be for a woman with Sabrina's qualifications to waste them—for her not to be an example to the young women of Vela and her own daughters.'

The old man shook his head. 'Never while I draw breath.'

The office was the second place Sebastian looked for her, and the sound of voices through the half-open door, or one voice in particular, told him he was in the right place.

He pushed open the door and was stopped in his tracks. On one side of the room his wife's PA stood weeping while Sabrina, her chin up, her eyes blazing, was facing a third woman he vaguely recognised—then he placed her. The tall brunette was Count Hugo's niece.

'What is happening?'

'Sebastian! This woman…' Teeth clenched, Sabrina looked at the tall brunette and took a deep breath. '*This* woman says she is my new assistant and I was telling her that I already have an assistant.'

'Highness, the workload has become too much for

Rachel, who is being reassigned to a less stressful position.' She held out a file she was holding and a memory stick. 'I have already made a start on the speech Her Highness is giving to the friends of the hospital. I have redrafted it into a more…acceptable form.'

Sabrina put her hands on her hips. 'What was wrong with it as it was?' she asked in a dangerous voice.

'It is a professional occasion. Certain things can be misinterpreted when taken out of context.'

While the other two women faced off, Sebastian went over to where the weeping girl stood and put his hand on her hunched, shaking shoulder. 'Do you find working for my wife stressful? You can be honest.' He exchanged a look with Sabrina. 'She can be difficult.'

The girl dashed a hand across her damp face and shook her head. 'No, I love working for the Princess. She is so kind and…' Her lips began to quiver again as she wailed, 'She's lovely.'

Sebastian nodded and turned back to Hugo's niece, who was regarding the weeping younger girl with distaste. 'It looks like there has been a mistake. As you see, my wife already has an assistant.'

'With the greatest of respect, Highness, the King himself has asked me to step in and, though I do not like to say it—'

'But you say it anyway—admirable. And I see a family trait.'

'Certain aspects of Rachel's work have been found unsatisfactory.'

'Not by me, they haven't!' Sabrina retorted.

'No, *cara*, what she means is that Rachel has not been passing on the information about you when requested.' He glanced towards Rachel, who sniffed and nodded. 'So,' he added, 'they decided to insert a more qualified spy.'

'I must protest…!'

Sebastian whipped around and fixed the woman with a stare of arctic contempt. 'Then do so out of my sight.'

Sabrina, whose inarticulate rage had been replaced by shock, watched, her mouth slightly open, as the woman, red-faced, walked from the room. 'What just happened?' she said faintly when the door closed.

Sebastian smiled at her and moved to where Rachel was drying her eyes.

'Does that mean I'm still working for Sa… the Princess?'

'It does.'

'But the King—'

'You work for Princess Sabrina, you answer to Princess Sabrina, and she is the *only* person who can dismiss you.'

Sabrina went across to where the girl stood. 'And I don't,' she said, giving the girl a hug.

'Now, Rachel, I will obviously defer to the boss here—' he glanced at Sabrina '—but I think you deserve the rest of the day off. Have a tissue, a box,' he added generously, handing the girl the box on the desk.

Rachel, receiving it, looked at Sabrina, who nodded. 'Yes, that will be fine, Rachel, thanks, and sorry.'

She waited until the door closed before turning to Sebastian.

'Thank you for that, but I could have handled it,' she added, just in case he thought she was pathetic.

'I never doubted it, but you shouldn't have needed to. I should have laid some ground rules with my father before I left…but I've done that now and I don't think there will be any more incidents like that.'

'You've spoken to him already…before…?' She stopped, lowering her eyes and thinking, *Of course he went to see his father first, Brina. You are not his first priority.*

'How was your trip?' He dragged a hand through his hair. 'It was pretty much like every other meeting I have attended—long…lots of time with nothing to do but think. I've been a fool.'

He took her face between his hands and paused, his eyes closing as he relived that moment of mind-numbing shock that had come after a week of denial and misery. A week spent wondering what she was doing, if she was all right, missing her voice, the smell of her skin, missing her! Fighting the knowledge that at some point Sabrina had crept into his heart, into his soul. Fighting because he was a coward, fighting what he ought to have been rejoicing, pushing her away when he ought to have been pulling her to him.

Sabrina saw the pain in his face and ached for him. It must have been a pretty catastrophic meeting to make him look like that. 'I'm sure you weren't.'

His soul-piercing blue eyes opened. 'I was… I am… I feel as though the earth has shifted beneath my feet. Nothing is… I used to be so *sure*…' Sure that love was a fool's game, sure that it was not for him and enjoying the smug sense of superiority and the false sense of security his tunnel vision had given him.

The fact that this mind-set might actually shut him off from one of life's greatest joys was not something he had ever considered.

'You remember something I said once? That it wouldn't happen to me…that I was not expecting to—?'

His words were like a blow she hadn't seen coming. They drained her face of colour, and she spoke quickly because she didn't want to hear him say it. 'You've met someone,' she said in a dead little voice.

It seemed ironic now that when she had overheard those gossiping bitches it had not even crossed her mind that they were telling the truth.

'I appreciate your honesty,' she lied, 'but I would prefer not to know her name.'

'What are you talking about?'

'You've fallen in love.' It was not a question; it explained the difference she sensed in him.

'Yes.'

She tried to pull away but the hands on her shoulders tightened. 'Look at me, Sabrina.'

'I can't. I hate you.'

'Has anyone ever told you you have the most incredible mouth?'

Her head slowly lifted; she looked up at him, tears trembling on her lashes. 'Why are you saying that?'

He stood there looking down at her feeling that he was standing on the brink of a precipice about to step out into the black unknown. It didn't make him the least bit fearful.

'And why are you looking at me like that?' She gasped, feeling her insides melt.

'Because you're incredible. Your skin is like cream.' He reached out, an expression of fascination stamped on his lean face as he let strands of caramel-streaked honey slip through his fingers. 'Have you any idea of how much of a turn-on it is to know that I can make you shake without even touching you?'

'But you are touching me.' Sabrina, her head spinning, let out a faint whimper as his hand moved to cup the soft curve of her cheek in his hand before rubbing his thumb across the plump lower lip of her Cupid's bow mouth. 'You love someone else.'

He shook his head. 'How could I when I can only see you? Your eyes are extraordinary.' He stood staring deep into the dark liquid depths framed by long curling lashes, waiting for them to darken with passion before he kissed her.

The kiss seemed to go on for ever, and when he lifted his head she felt as though she were floating.

'You are my life. I love you.'

'I love you, Sebastian…' Her whispered echo was barely audible above the clamouring beat of her heart.

CHAPTER TWELVE

THE KISS WAS deep and so tender that there were tears in her eyes when he finally lifted his head.

'The first thing I remember is your mouth and kissing you in the car.'

'You were cruel,' she remembered. 'And drunk.'

'Not really, but I do remember that you looked at me like I was the devil so I played it up a bit.' His eyes darkened as he curled his fingers round her chin and turned her face up to him. 'But all the time I was thinking about your mouth.'

She swallowed, feeling dizzy, happiness bubbling up inside her. Could this really be happening? 'Thinking what?'

'That it was a total miracle and many...so many things I wanted to do to and with it, and I thought of my brother having that mouth and I wanted to—' His hand fell away and he inhaled. 'I felt like hell.' He gave a twisted smile. 'Because as you probably realised the honourable stuff is not a natural fit for me. Every time I looked at you I wanted to taste you and every time I tasted you I wanted to do it again, but you belonged to Luis.

'When he dumped you at the altar I was furious with him—for about ten seconds. Then I was glad, because there was nothing stopping me from having you.'

She lifted a hand to his cheek. He turned his face into it and kissed her palm as she stood there, tears streaming down her face as the words poured out of him.

His blue eyes blazed fiercely, bathing her in the love that shone in them as he took both her hands in his and, bending forward, kissed her again. This time the tenderness tipped over into hunger that made her knees give way.

Sebastian reacted by picking her up and carrying her over to the sofa in the corner of the room, and after pulling her across his knees he carried on kissing her.

Then minutes later, breathing hard, several items of clothing on the floor, she pressed her hand on his chest and shook her head.

'Why…why now? I've been crazy about you for weeks and weeks and you…couldn't you see that I loved you?'

The breath caught in her throat at the look in his eyes. 'Say that again!' he demanded fiercely.

'I love you, Sebastian.'

He smiled, the fierce tenderness in his face making her head spin as he curved a hand around one side of her face, taking his time to taste every inch of her face before pausing, his nose pressed to the side of hers, their warm breath mingling.

'You were with me out of duty, not choice. I never forgot that, and I have gone through life telling myself that love was a mugs' game, I didn't believe in it, but the truth is,' he admitted heavily, clenching his teeth as the full level of his stupidity was laid bare for her, 'I was scared of feeling anything that much. I watched the person I cared for most in the world destroyed by love…'

'Your mother…' she breathed, her voice soft with sympathy.

He nodded. 'I judged her and I was helpless to help her. I never wanted to love anyone again and let them down.' He gave a hard laugh. 'I *really* thought that there was choice involved and then *you* happened. I have learnt so much being with you and I swear that I'll always be there—'

She pressed a finger to his lips. 'Don't swear—kiss.'

With a growl he responded to the imperious little command and, tipping her under him, he gathered her to him and proceeded to kiss her senseless in the process, losing his own sense also.

As she moved in his arms and almost fell off the narrow couch her eyes caught sight of the clock on the wall. 'Oh, my God, look at the time!' she exclaimed. 'There's no need to look so smug.'

'I feel smug.' He felt...*complete*.

'We've been here all afternoon, Seb. We need to get dressed for dinner.'

She was about to draw her legs up to her chin when his hand went to the smooth naked curve of her bottom. 'You look like a little cat when you stretch.'

'Seb!' she pleaded, struggling to inject some reproach and not only throaty appeal into her voice. 'Dinner...' She felt a little slug of disappointment when he reacted to the reminder and sat upright.

Sabrina followed suit, mentally calculating how quickly they could make themselves presentable for the formal dinner awaiting them and get back to their suite without anyone noticing how dishevelled they both looked.

'Should I ring down and tell them we'll be late dining?'

'Don't bother. I've already dealt with that.' He stretched

to ease the kinks out of his spine, drawing her eyes to the perfect muscular development of his lean torso. Everything about his body delighted her.

'You're totally…' Their eyes connected; emotion rose in her chest, consolidating into a knot of sheer longing. She had never in her life imagined that loving someone could feel like this, that it could be so all-consuming and the physical aspect so incredible.

And he loved her back…it still felt as though she were living a dream.

'Looking for these?' He picked a pair of lacy pants from the table on her side of the sofa and tossed them to her, feeling his libido kick in hard as she straightened and raised a hand, causing her firm breasts to jiggle and sway as she caught them.

'How organised—and when?'

'While you were snoring.'

'I do not snore!'

'I shall invest in a set of earplugs.' His eyes were warm as he levered himself lazily from the tumbled bed, reaching for his boxers.

Sabrina watched the play of muscle gliding and bunching under the golden skin of his back as he stood with his back to her pulling his jeans on over his narrow hips.

God, but he was beautiful!

Hand in hand, they walked up the rear staircase that led to their bedroom suite; the sitting-room door was not closed. Inside two maids bobbed curtsies as they entered before one pushed a trolley with a cloth thrown over up to one of the sofas in the room and the other plugged in the large flatscreen TV that rested on the second trolley.

'We'll serve ourselves, thank you.'

The maids nodded and vanished.

Sabrina watched as Sebastian lifted the cloth with a flourish to reveal silver domes, which he lifted to inspect the food underneath, filling the room with smells that made her realise how hungry she was.

'We are going to eat on trays and watch *television*?' she said, thinking, *How crazy is this?* She was feeling the sort of excited incredulity that most women would if their husband said that he'd arranged for them to eat food created by a Michelin-starred chef served on antique china sitting at a table loaded with silver and crystal.

But in her world this was a treat.

'Isn't it what people do?'

She nodded, thinking that Sebastian was a billion miles from other people; he was extraordinary!

'I thought you might like a night off.'

She nodded vigorously.

'Movie's your choice, so kick off your shoes—'

She looked down, a smile tugging at her lips as she realised she had walked barefoot down the corridor. 'I'm not wearing any.'

They had just sat down when the door opened; without warning a figure scanned the room before the King walked in.

When he saw the TV and the trays he could not have looked more shocked had he walked in and found them rolling around on the floor naked. Half an hour earlier and he might have, she thought, hiding a grin.

'Father.' Sebastian got to his feet slowly, his casual attitude thinly masking his anger. Seeing it there just below the surface, Sabrina felt her heart sink like a stone. 'Sorry, if we'd known you were coming we'd have saved you some.'

'You would possibly have dressed for dinner too?' The King took a deep breath and shook his head. 'No, it is none of my business. I accept that things change. I have come to apologise,' he said stiffly. 'Some…most of the things you said were right. You are doing a good job. I should have said it before but I… It is hard not to feel needed.

'Your brother—if he and his family wish to come to the reunification ceremony then I will be glad to see them as my guests. And, Sabrina, I have no objection to you working, and, yes, I agree it will be a good example to set to your daughters and the young women of our country.' He inclined his head. 'So I will say goodnight.'

'What,' Sabrina gasped as the door closed, 'was that?'

'That, my dearest darling, was hell freezing over— with style, to give the devil his due,' he added wryly. 'Now, where were we?'

Sabrina shook her head and pushed him away as he leaned in to kiss her. 'Luis? Me working? What was all that about?'

'When I went to Paris it wasn't for a meeting—I was seeing Luis.'

She drew back, startled. 'Luis?'

'Do you mind?'

'Why would I mind? I would actually love to thank him for dumping me at the altar considering how things have worked out.'

Sebastian grinned. 'So you'd have no problem with him coming to the reunification ceremony next year?'

'And your father agreed?'

'That was quite a climb-down. And quick,' he admitted. 'But I think it is the idea of a baby—'

'Luis is having a baby?' she exclaimed.

'Well, not Luis—but, yes, and I think that might be the swing vote. I'm starting to think that Father is getting a little soft in his old age.'

Sabrina gave a sceptical grunt. 'That is only one part of the mystery. What about me working?'

'I think he has decided that to have talent in the family firm and not utilise it is a waste—especially when the research is so important.'

'He has decided?' She shook her head. 'What have you been up to, Seb?'

'Me?' he said, looking innocent. 'I had nothing to do with it except to mention the need for further research into dementia and expertise right here.'

'Oh, my God—truly? Me, work?' She began to bounce excitedly.

'I expect you'll be running the university in a few years.'

'If having those daughters he was talking about doesn't get in the way.'

'What can I say? He's keen on grandchildren.'

She smiled and looked at him, eyes gleaming through her lashes as she straddled him.

'And how do you feel about children?'

'Pretty damn good so long as you're the mother.' He let out a low growl and tugged her down onto him. 'How do you feel about starting now? I've heard it can take a while.'

'In that case, less talk more action, hmm?'

'Shut up, woman, can't you see I'm dynasty-building?'

There was very little talking for some time, but a *lot* of communicating.

EPILOGUE

SEBASTIAN WAS THE last to speak. He kept it short.

'I feel that the people here today to celebrate the day our country becomes one have already said it.'

He gestured with a flourish towards his father and the Duke, who were seated on the stage, and there was a cheer from the crowds that filled the palace parkland as far as the eye could see.

'I have only one thing to add. A wise man once said...' he smiled at his father '...that it is all about family.' He moved to the edge of the stage and held out a hand to his brother, who sat with his wife and baby in the front row.

Luis jumped up on the stage to a loud cheer.

Sebastian put his arm around his brother.

'And today our family, our country, has expanded in a beautiful way, a little like my lovely wife.'

It was Luis, along with Chloe, who pulled Sabrina, heavily pregnant, to her feet and escorted her over to Sebastian before clapping his hands and backing away to leave them centre stage.

The applause was thunderous as Sebastian kissed his wife on the lips, his grin flashing.

'You promised you wouldn't do this.'

He shrugged. 'My memory, darling, it is not what it once was.'

She dabbed the emotional tears running down her cheeks and began to laugh while the crowds cheered on, but she had the last laugh.

'If my waters break right here and now it won't be pretty.'

He leaned in close and whispered, 'Everything you do, my love, is *beautiful*!'

The reunification of Vela was also the birthday of the future King—the people said it was a very good omen...

* * * * *

If you enjoyed A RING TO SECURE HIS CROWN, why not explore these other Kim Lawrence stories?

*SURRENDERING TO THE
ITALIAN'S COMMAND
ONE NIGHT TO WEDDING VOWS
HER NINE MONTH CONFESSION
THE SINS OF SEBASTIAN REY-DEFOE
ONE NIGHT WITH MORELLI*

Available now!